SURVIVOR GIRL

by Erin Teagan

CLARION BOOKS

HOUGHTON MIFFLIN HARCOURT

BOSTON   NEW YORK

Clarion Books
3 Park Avenue
New York, New York 10016

Clarion Books is an imprint of Houghton Mifflin Harcourt Publishing Company.

hmhco.com

The text was set in Sabon MT Std.

Library of Congress Cataloging-in-Publication Data
Names: Teagan, Erin, author.
Title: Survivor girl / by Erin Teagan.
Description: Boston ; New York : Clarion Books, Houghton Mifflin Harcourt, [2019] |
Summary: Twelve-year-old Ali is unsure about joining her brother and their reality-show
celebrity father, Survivor Guy, on location and disappointed when she learns how much of the
show is fake, but heroic when wildfire strikes.
Identifiers: LCCN 2018051978 (print) | LCCN 2018056565 (ebook) |
ISBN 9780544635364 (E-book) | ISBN 9780544636217 (hardback)
Subjects: | CYAC: Reality television programs—Fiction. | Television programs—Production
and direction—Fiction. | Survival—Fiction. | Self-confidence—Fiction. | Divorce—Fiction. |
BISAC: JUVENILE FICTION / Humorous Stories. | JUVENILE FICTION / Social Issues
/ Self-Esteem & Self-Reliance. | JUVENILE FICTION / Family / Marriage & Divorce. |
JUVENILE FICTION / Family / Siblings. | JUVENILE FICTION / Social Issues / Friendship.
| JUVENILE FICTION / Sports & Recreation / Camping & Outdoor Activities. | JUVENILE
FICTION / Nature & the Natural World / General (see also headings under Animals).
| JUVENILE FICTION / Action & Adventure / Survival Stories.Classification: LCC
PZ7.1.T424 (ebook) | LCC PZ7.1.T424 Sur 2019 (print) |
DDC [Fic]—dc23
LC record available at https://lccn.loc.gov/2018051978

Printed in the United States of America
DOC 10 9 8 7 6 5 4 3 2 1
4500761006

For Cailin, my littlest sister,
who is always up for an adventure

ONE

It's after midnight when I hear his car in the driveway and I stumble out of bed.

"Ow!"

"Oh! Sorry!" I say, forgetting my best friend is asleep in the trundle bed next to me.

She sits up, rubbing an elbow. "Your dad?"

I press my face against the window and see the Jeep, illuminated in the spotlights above our garage. Green and red, a snorkel attached to the hood, nets and snake traps strapped to the top, and a bungee cord holding a container of gas to the bumper. "He's home." I try to whisper, because it's best if Mom doesn't know yet since—officially—he was supposed to be home in time for my sixth-grade graduation earlier that night. But when you're dealing with time zones and monster alligators and life and death, can you really be expected to keep appointments?

"Your mom's going to kill him. I'm out of here," Harper says, sliding into her flip-flops.

I swear I see movement in one of the cages tied to the roof rack. Snake? Mongoose? Kitten? Harper wedges in next to me at the window.

"Put your bag down," I say. "Mom will never let you leave."

The door to the Jeep pops open and Dad steps onto the driveway. It's like a thousand-pound weight is lifted off my back. He's home. He's safe. But then my idiot brother, Jake, slides out of the back door of the car, his arm in a sling, limping across the driveway. Harper gasps, but honestly, is it really a surprise that Jake comes back injured every time?

"Alison?" Mom calls from her bedroom.

"It's Dad," I say, bolting out of my room and down the stairs.

Before I can even get to the kitchen, Harper skidding after me, the door to the garage bursts open and there stand Dad and Jake, mud-streaked and sunburned. Dad lifts me up and tosses me in the air like I'm two instead of twelve. "Ali-Gator!" he says, nearly squeezing the organs out of me.

"Can we not say that word?" Jake moans. His khaki sling looks like it was made out of an old pair of cargo shorts.

"Hi, Jake," Harper says in her girly voice she usually saves for Brad Garrison. It's disgusting. Dad's been letting Jake go on shoots for his show, *Survivor Guy*, ever since he graduated high school last year, and now Harper thinks he's some kind of celebrity. I keep reminding her he's the same kid who crashed his car into the garage a few months ago.

Dad shakes his head. "You'll be fine, Jake. It was only a baby. FACT!" he says and points a finger at him. "They almost never carry diseases."

"Where have you been?" I ask. "I thought you were in Saskatchewan."

Jake shifts his arm in the sling, cringing. "Louisiana bayou."

"You missed graduation," Harper pipes in, putting an arm around my shoulder.

I push her away. How could she say that? My dad just came all the way from the bayou, where Jake practically lost his arm to an alligator. What better reason than 'I saved my own son from the vicious jaws of a man-eating reptile?' Excuse accepted, in my book.

"Production went over, Ali." Dad drops his three-hundred-pound backpack in the kitchen, pots and spoons and fishing nets clattering to the floor. "Where's your mom?"

I point upstairs and Harper starts to head toward the door. "Will you knock it off?" I say. "She'll be happy to see he's okay." But I know she's probably fuming. It's like she doesn't even get that Survivor Guys have a commitment to the wilderness. And sometimes that means sacrifice.

Dad climbs the stairs, his hiking boots leaving crumbs of dirt on the carpet. "Michelle?"

We stand in silence for a moment, Jake picking at his sling.

"You could have called, you know." I cross my arms. "We were worried."

Jake rolls his eyes. "Sure, next time I'm wrangling mosquitoes the size of bats and losing half my arm to an alligator, I'll whip out my phone and give you a call." He snorts and so does Harper. Traitor. How could she think Jake is anything but seriously disgusting? I know for a fact he never changes his socks.

"Can we go back to bed now?" Harper asks, yawning. "It's like one in the morning."

I yawn too, my body suddenly heavy with exhaustion.

"I got most-improved player at the archery banquet," I say to Jake as we all head up the stairs.

"What? No you didn't," Harper says.

"Well, I almost did," I reply. "Coach said I was the runner-up most-improved while you were in the bathroom."

"Aren't you the only person on the team?" Jake laughs at his own joke.

I flick him in the back of the neck. "Harper's on the team too." But to be honest, the team was pretty pathetic. We spent most of our time slurping down the blueberry-vanilla smoothies our coach brought from his side job at the smoothie stand downtown. My mouth waters.

Dad appears at the top of the stairs, stretching. "Well, that's it for me tonight. Time to hit the hay."

He passes us on his way down, stopping to squeeze Jake's alligator-bite arm. "Ow!"

"FACT," Dad says. "That means it's healing."

Harper and I glance at each other because we're pretty sure that's not a fact. But Dad's tired and probably half delirious from the long drive. He kisses me on the forehead and flashes a thumbs-up to Harper. "See you kids tomorrow." I watch him leave through the front door.

"Where's he going?" Harper asks.

"Probably left something in the Jeep," I say.

Jake looks at me. "He's going to a hotel."

"What? Why?" Harper says, struggling to catch up with us on the stairs.

"He hasn't lived here for like three months," Jake says. "That's what happens when parents—"

"Is that a tick on your leg?" I say, then barrel past him and into my room, Harper trailing me.

I turn off the light and dig myself under the covers.

"I thought we told each other everything," Harper says in the darkness.

I peek out of my blanket and see she's sitting up on her bed in the tiny bit of moonlight coming through the window. Behind her, my shelves are overflowing with books on survival: *How to Fight off a Bear, The Essential Guide to Poisonous Plants, How to Treat a*

Jellyfish Sting on a Deserted Island, and a thousand more. I sleep with the most important one under my pillow: *A Survivalist's Guide.* Written by my own grandpa, General Frederick D. Kensington.

"You were the first person I told when Peaches died," Harper continues.

I groan, kicking my covers off. "It's just temporary. A short separation." The word burns my throat. "Barely worth mentioning."

"I even told you about my wart." She lies back down, out of sight.

"There's nothing to tell, Harper. Really." I roll over and hang off the edge of the bed. "It's just since my dad's show got picked up by a TV network, it's doing really well. So, he's barely home."

She pulls her blankets up and turns away from me.

"He has his own bear spray brand, you know. Survive-A-Bear."

Silence.

"Comes in pink."

"It's all about honesty, Alison," Harper says, still facing away from me. "Dr. Tom says if you can't be honest with yourself, then you can't be honest with anyone else."

Dr. Tom is the head of our Healthy Is Happy! afterschool club, which we'd almost been kicked out of twice for smuggling root beer barrels onto the activity bus. Apparently they're made out of pure evil and will rot your teeth and the rest of your insides before you can even cry for help.

"Dr. Tom wears socks with his sandals. I thought we weren't taking him seriously," I reply.

Harper burrows deeper into her bed with an angry flick of her blankets.

My stomach grumbles and I wish I had a root beer barrel right now, because actually they're not evil, but pure sugar goodness. Perfect for getting out the sour taste I suddenly have in my mouth.

"Well, good night," I say. Harper doesn't answer.

I throw myself back onto my pillow, my head hitting something hard. I reach underneath and pull out my survival book and something new that hadn't been there before. It's a beat-up box, taped together and layered in dirt. When I was really little, Dad used to leave coins and feathers and beads under my pillow when he got back in the middle of the night from his trips, so I know it's from him.

A plume of dust settles on my bed as I try to open

the box. I brush the dirt from my sheets, pulling the tape apart more carefully. This could be anything: dried-up flowers; seeds; fabric; a living, breathing animal. Dad's not the best gift-giver, but like my mom always says, it's the thought that counts.

I open the box all the way, and take out the trinket nestled inside. It's a mudded-up compass. I pick off the dried mosquito stuck to its face and turn it over. There's a message scratched into the back, and it says FOREVER MY SURVIVOR GIRL. HAPPY GRADUATION.

I knew he didn't forget.

TWO

I wake up early the next morning and Dad's already standing on the ladder on the back of his Jeep pulling crates and cages off his roof rack. I swipe a leaf off the giant picture of him on the driver's side door advertising SURVIVOR GUY—ONE MAN. ONE CAMERA. MILES OF UNFORGIVING WILDERNESS. TUNE IN FOR THE ADVENTURE! SUNDAYS 8 P.M.

"Can you grab this for me?" he says, handing down a rusted-out crate with something flopping inside. I flinch away, then realize it's only another leaf.

"No problem." I stack it on top of the growing tower teetering into the rosebushes.

"I got doughnuts. Help yourself." He motions toward the bag of deliciousness balancing on his back bumper.

I choose the one with the most sprinkles.

"Thanks for the compass, Dad. I love it," I say, my mouth full, reaching up for another crate.

"I'm proud of you, Ali-Gator." He unties some rope on the roof and flings it onto the driveway. "Heard you're doing great in soccer, too."

"Archery," I correct him. "I got most-improved player." Harper flip-flops out of the garage with her overnight bag. "At least, I almost did."

She waves to me as she walks across the driveway and onto her front lawn next door.

"Where are you going?" I ask.

"Home." She doesn't even look back.

"Look, doughnuts!" I call after her, because Mom never lets me have this kind of food around the house. Normally it's plain yogurt and granola for breakfast. She's a nutritionist and she takes her job way too seriously. Dad is all danger and fun and you-only-live-once. Mom is food diaries, vitamins, and ice-cream-is-the-devil.

There's no answer from Harper, and I know from

the berserk barking of her dogs that she's already through her door.

I feel like stomping right over there and banging on her perfect door with its perfect WELCOME, FRIENDS wreath her mom made by hand. I know for a fact she doesn't tell me everything. Like the time she ate all the marshmallows out of the cereal and left me with only the oaty triangles. And I'm such a good friend, I didn't even say anything.

"Ali? Here." Dad hands me another cage and I place it on top of the rest. An old car drives slowly past our house, and I wish we could go inside. Sometimes the *Survivor Guy* stalkers really get to me.

Not Dad though. He wants all the attention he can get for his show. He shakes out a net, revealing a massive gaping hole. "Badger," he says loudly toward the road. "Bit right through the darn thing." He crumples it up and throws it into the corner of the garage.

"He's gone, Dad," I say.

Every once in a while, I'll see paparazzi hanging out in the neighborhood with their fancy extendo cameras. Dad's in newspapers and magazines all the time. Lately it's been about his new bear spray and how it sold out of Outdoor Land stores in one week. The last time I was in a magazine was a summer ago when Dad and I ate breakfast at the pond behind the nature center where Mom likes to run. "Celebrities Do Everyday Things: They Eat Pop-Tarts."

Mom comes out of the house dragging her suitcase, the screen door smacking closed behind her.

She's smiling, and a maybe-bubble forms in my belly. Like, maybe she'll be nice to Dad. Maybe they won't fight. But then she stops in her tracks, her smile tightening. She plucks the last bite of doughnut right out of my hand. "Really, George?" And then tosses it into the garbage can.

My maybe-bubble pops.

"Try not to eat all junk while I'm gone, okay?" she says.

"Where are you going?" Dad asks, and I knew this was going to happen. I should have reminded him immediately when he got home last night.

Mom crosses her arms, mad as usual. "My conference, George. Nutritionists Unite? I'm the keynote speaker?" She groans. "We've had this on our calendar since Thanksgiving."

Dad wipes his brow. "Oh, right, yes, yes." But I can see it in his eyes, the way they dart from me to the house to the half-unpacked Jeep. He forgot.

"You have Alison the whole week. I won't be back until Thursday night." She shakes her head at him like he's the worst dad on the planet. "Don't let Jake use the weed whacker, okay, Alison? And call whenever you want, don't worry about your minutes." She tries to hug me but I turn away from her and fold my arms.

If there's a week when Dad's home, we should be doing things together as a family. We should be making homemade pizzas and drinking sodas in the kitchen like they do on that commercial. But I know Mom won't understand. She never gets anything anymore.

"Michelle," Dad says. "I, uh—"

"Don't even." Mom picks up her bag, rolling her eyes. "I know you forgot, but I'm just going to pretend you didn't, because this conference is important and—"

"I can go to Harper's house," I say. "For the weekend. She's not speaking to me, but I don't mind."

"Would that be okay?" Dad asks and Mom drops

her bag like she's ready for a brawl right here on the driveway. I check the road for extendo cameras.

"Michelle," Dad says, stiffening. "I've got a production schedule, give me a break."

And then I remember Harper's going fishing with her father. "Actually, never mind, um—"

But my parents have hustled themselves into the Jeep, shutting the doors and rolling up all the windows, and I'm just talking to myself. That's what they do. Find someplace to hide while they fight, except they forget that the Jeep is made mostly out of canvas. I look at the road some more, pretending I don't hear Mom yelling at Dad for not spending any time with me and missing my graduation, and she's really letting him have it. I want to open the Jeep doors and save him, but when I take a step closer, my mom wags a warning finger at me and they start to whisper. I spin in the other direction and kick rocks into the garden until they emerge. A united front.

Dad's smiling, and Mom still looks peeved. "So, my Ali-Gator," Dad says, clapping his hands. "You still reading those survival books?"

"Every one in the library," I say, and it's not an exaggeration.

Mom's taxi pulls into the driveway.

"What do you say about putting all that reading into action and coming on set with me and Jake this week?" Dad says. "It's our season finale. A big one."

"What?" It's Jake, still in his pajamas, touching all the doughnuts, a tiny Band-Aid on his arm that's no longer in a sling. Typical Jake to make such a big deal about an injury the size of a paper cut. "She's coming with us?"

My body feels like it's on fire. I should be happy about this. It's what I've always wanted, to follow in the shoes of the General and my dad. The first Survivor Girl. It's in my blood, right? But the truth is, I've never actually eaten a grasshopper for breakfast or slept in a tent made of seaweed. And maybe I've never even started a campfire with a hair band and a nail file like I told all my friends.

"Aren't there laws about kids on TV shows?" I say. "I wouldn't want to break the law or anything."

"Nonsense!" Dad says.

I look up at Harper's bedroom window, the shades closed tight. If she's mad at me for not telling her about my dad staying in a hotel for one night, she'll ditch me for good once she finds out I'm a survivalist fake. So will all my other friends. "But, Dad, I'm only twelve—"

And before I even finish my sentence I know what he's going to say. "I was only thirteen when I survived that boat accident off the coast of Australia with my parents and then got lost out at sea for three nights and two days and survived by befriending the hungry sharks and manta rays." Because I've heard that story at least five thousand times, not to mention read it in about three hundred newspapers. Once, it was even reenacted in a Nat Geo special, *Me and My Manta Ray*. It's basically how he got so famous.

Mom drops her wheelie bag. "Forget it. I'm staying home. You're not going anywhere, Ali." She strides over, taking me by the elbow.

I pull away from her. "No. Wait. I want to go."

"Nope," she says with a huff. "What if something happens to you out there?"

"She'll be fine, Michelle," Dad says, balling up another net and stuffing it into a bag. "She's my Survivor Girl."

"That's not the only thing I'm worried about." She stares at Dad meaningfully, and then they're having some kind of telepathic fight with their eyeballs.

"Stop it!" I say. "I'm going with Dad."

Mom leans into my face. "There are things you don't understand, Ali. I'm just protecting you."

Protecting me. It's something she says all the time now. Protecting me from getting a stomachache, protecting me from bad skin, protecting me from an injury.

"No," I say. "I'm going with Dad. I'm not a baby anymore, Mom."

"Let her come, Michelle," Dad says. "You can't control everything."

The taxi driver beeps his horn. "I'm not the one trying to control everything, George." She turns to me after a dirty look to Dad. "I'm just saying, sweetheart, that you might not be ready for this."

"Dad's right. Stop being so controlling."

Mom steps away from me. "Alison, you don't even know what you're saying." I expect her face to be angry, lips pursed, eyes squinty mad. The way her face is almost all the time lately. But when I look up, she won't even make eye contact with me.

"Well, I still love you, Mom!" Jake says, laughing, punching me in the shoulder like this is all some funny joke.

Mom clears her throat and picks up the handle of her suitcase. She tries to hug me again and I back away, even though I don't mean to.

"Call me if you need me, Ali. Anytime. I love you."

But I can't find my voice to tell her I love her back. My stomach jumbled, I hear her walk to the taxi, one of the wheels of her suitcase squealing. Broken.

And then I watch the taxi drive past the Rickles' house and the school bus stop. I watch until it turns the corner and heads toward the main road.

"What was that about?" Jake says too loudly. "Way to make Mom cry, Ali."

"No I didn't." I pinch him on the arm.

"Yes you did."

"No I didn't!"

"FACT!" Dad says. "Mother-daughter relationships are as complicated as the wilderness."

My body tingles with panic. The wilderness. My first appearance on *Survivor Guy,* and I'm going to blow it.

Dad's jostling me around now like he used to when I was five, his face bright. "Cheer up! We're going to have a blast." He bangs me on the back. "Pack your bags! Great Dismal Swamp, here we come!"

"Great dismal what?" I say.

"Great Dismal Swamp!" he repeats. "Get ready to be SUR-viiiiiived!"

Harper's face appears in one of her windows and she scowls. The tower of crates behind me shifts, wobbles, and collapses onto the driveway with a clatter.

THREE

We spend the next hour packing our bags and organizing the Jeep, restocking the bug spray and filling tanks with water. My stomach gurgles with anxiety. In all of my survivor books, I've never come across anything about the Great Dismal Swamp.

Even worse, when I text Harper that I'm going away with my dad, she doesn't even answer.

"What if I make a fool of myself in front of the camera?" I say.

"It's just another swamp," Dad says. "We were supposed to be going to Antarctica, but the guide got sick. Swamps are easy. If you can avoid the deadly critters, there's plenty of shelter from the elements and food to forage."

My friends think I've cooked a snake over a campfire and made a mattress out of leaves and moss. They think my dad takes me on crazy father-daughter expeditions over school breaks. Last Thanksgiving, when Harper went to her Uncle's wedding in California and half our friends were gone visiting family, I told everyone he taught me how to navigate a sailboat by the North Star alone. And they believed me. Why wouldn't they? I'm Survivor Guy's daughter.

Dad's picking bugs off the grill of his Jeep now, talking into his phone. The truth is, he's so busy being a famous survivalist, we've never been on a father-daughter expedition. Not even one.

Jake stumbles out of the garage and tosses his bag into the Jeep. "I call the back." He crawls in and splays across both seats.

"What kind of elements?" I say, looking at my own duffel bag, which is half the size of Jake's.

"You'll be fine, Alison," Dad says. "I have everything you need."

"I brought the chocolate raisins," Jake says.

"Do you have snake-bite kits?" I ask. "Sunblock? Oh wait, I forgot something."

Jake groans, then sits and buckles up. "Are you going to be like this the whole trip?"

Dad takes my bag and I run back inside. My room is still a mess from my sleepover with Harper, sheets and blankets everywhere. Empty wrappers from the butterscotch candies that we snuck from Harper's house are crinkled on the floor. I hide the evidence in the trash, grab the General's book from beneath my pillow, and rush back outside.

As I climb into the car, I look into the windows of Harper's house. Does she see me? Does she know I'm being dragged off to a dismal swamp to survive with Survivor Guy himself for the whole week?

"Dad," I say. "Maybe I should stay at Harper's. Her dad's taking her fishing, but they'd probably let me go along." I clear my throat, my stomach seizing up as we pull away from my house with my books and my hermit crab called Sandy and my real bed not made out of spiderwebs and leaves. "I mean, I can't let Harper spend her first week of summer vacation without me."

Jake makes a baby-crying noise and I reach around my seat to cause him some serious facial damage, except Dad grabs my hand.

"Sit down," he says. "You're ready. You have the will and the knowledge and—FACT!—that is all you need to survive the elements. Plus, don't you remember fending off that angry buffalo in first grade?"

"It was a golden retriever, Dad," I say, and Jake snickers.

Dad pats me on the shoulder. "The details don't matter much. You have the survivor instinct. It's in your blood!"

In all honesty, I don't have the will and probably not even the right kind of knowledge, and I certainly have never felt a survivor instinct of any sort.

"I don't think I should be on camera, Dad," I try, because if I get on camera, that means I will be on TV, and that means everyone will see me in all my survivalist glory. And by survivalist glory, I'm talking about stumbling into ravines or walking through a swarm of bees or throwing up when I have to eat my first meal of grasshoppers and frog legs. "I could, like, be your assistant off to the side or something while you and Jake make fires and leap canyons and stuff."

"Why are we bringing her?" Jake says from the back seat.

Dad shushes him with a wave of his hand. "Sweetie. Stop worrying so much. You're my Survivor Girl. You were born ready for this."

I watch as we pass the ice cream place where Harper and I always get black-raspberry swirl with extra rainbow sprinkles. We pass the music shop and the thrift store that puts survival books aside for me at the counter. I don't remind Dad that I got none of his survivor genes. That I'm allergic to mosquitoes and once when I got poison ivy raking leaves, I was bedridden for days. That I prefer air conditioning and cushy blankets and seeing the stars through my skylights rather than through the flap of a tent.

I definitely don't tell him that I've convinced everyone at school that I'm the next Survivor Girl, that as soon as I turn eighteen I'm joining the show, or maybe even starting a new one that's harder and more dangerous. Truth is, I don't have any business going anywhere near a swamp. Dismal or not.

FOUR

"First stop!" Dad announces, swinging us into a gas station.

The place is crawling with people. An archway of balloons is set up next to the car wash, a sign — BRAIN DISEASE! RAISE AWARENESS! FIND A CURE! — hanging from its center.

"What's this?" Jake asks.

"Looks like a ten-K run or something," Dad says, hopping out and stretching. "Too bad we don't have our running shoes, or we could join them."

"Yeah, too bad," I say.

Jake laughs. "Like you've ever run a mile in your life."

"Yes I have." And it's not even a good comeback because it's a lie. But I'm out of comeback practice since Jake's barely home anymore either.

Dad's taking an awfully long time pumping the gas, and the leather seat's sticking to my legs and arms in the beating sun. I wonder if the Great Dismal Swamp is hot in the middle of June and pull out Grandpa's guide. I'm reading the chapter on swamps when a guy wearing a T-shirt that says RUNNING IS MY LIFE! and a belt holding a bunch of little water bottles jogs up. "Are you by chance Survivor Guy?"

Dad turns to him. "Depends who's asking." He strikes a pose to match the giant sticker of himself on the side of the Jeep. And then they both laugh hysterically.

I fan my face with my book. Jake pushes against the back of my seat. "Get comfortable. We're going to be here awhile."

"I've always wondered," the runner says, "on episode thirty-four when you face that grizzly bear and his fangs are showing and his vicious claws are like inches from your face, how did you know to whistle that way?"

Dad rocks back on his heels and lets out an ear-piercing whistle that almost makes me drop my book. The cluster of runners by the car wash go silent and turn around. "That's the one!" the guy says. And then he mimes to the rest of the runners that Dad is in fact the real Survivor Guy. Even Dad looks alarmed as the entire clump marches over, phones ready to get a good picture.

I want to crawl into the back of the Jeep, but Jake has his rotten feet spreading foot fungus all over the seat next to him. I slump down instead, closing my guidebook.

"One at a time! One at a time!" Dad is grinning, pointing to the various *Survivor Guy* paraphernalia on the roof of the Jeep. "Yes, yes, that fishing spear is one hundred percent authentic bamboo from the legendary Hawaiian leper colony, Kalaupapa. Had to ride a mule down a cliff for that one."

Jake rips open a pepperoni stick and the Jeep is filled with the smell of smoked meat. I gag and try to open the door. But fans are clustered all around us to take pictures with Dad. "Excuse me," I call. "Survivor Girl coming through."

There's just enough space for me to suck in my

belly and slide out the door. I push my way through to Dad.

"... and then the camel just took off and thank goodness I had that helmet cam on because ..."

I pull on his shirt. "Dad? Don't we have a timeline?"

"... and I found myself in the middle of the Sahara Desert with no water or ..."

"Dad?" I pinch him in the arm. "I'm going to get some supplies in the store."

He's too engrossed in his story to notice me, so I pull his wallet out of his back pocket and weave through the crowd.

The blast of air conditioning feels as good as a black-raspberry swirl with extra rainbow sprinkles in the middle of August. I just soak it up until I hear the door jingle behind me as someone else comes in. First stop, slushy machine.

There's no line, so I step right up to the orange fizz pizzazz and fill my cup, ignoring my mother's voice in my head nagging me about the effects of sugar on my delicate complexion. I slurp the overflow around the edges and push the top on, spraying myself. I lunge for the napkin dispenser, orange fizz dripping from my hair, but someone's in my way.

"Alison?"

It's Brad Garrison, which is just plain fabulous.

"Hey, Brad," I say, all cool like I don't mind the orange slushy rolling down my cheek. I reach around him, manage to dislodge a stack of napkins two inches thick, and swipe at it.

"Are you here with your dad?" he asks.

"Yep, and my brother." I dab some napkins onto my shirt, but the damage is already done. "Just getting this for him," I say, holding up my slushy, "because, like, who drinks slushies at ten o' clock in the morning, right?"

He doesn't even hear me—he's on tiptoes to see over the shelves of bread and hot dog rolls to my dad's Jeep.

"So, are you running today in the race?" I ask. He's wearing an Autumn Leaf Middle School tank top with a giant number pinned to his back. Twenty-three. "That's my lucky number." What am I even saying? I need to get out of here. Something about Brad makes me stupid.

"What?" he says, looking down at his shirt. "Oh, yeah, running."

I grab a bag of trail mix and head for the cashier.

"Well, I'll see you later. Don't want to be late to the shoot."

Brad stops me. "You're going on a shoot? With Survivor Guy?"

I nod. "I guess he needs my expertise on this one. I know a lot about surviving in the wild. As you probably already know."

"That's so cool!" he says. "You're so lucky. I'd do anything to go on a trip with Survivor Guy."

"It takes years of preparation."

The cashier takes my money and I grab my stuff. Look at me, buying trail mix. A few chunks of walnut and some sesame seeds are all I need to survive in the wild.

"Where are you headed?" Brad asks, throwing his protein bar onto the counter. "A deserted island? The Canadian Rockies? I think my favorite show was when he parachuted into Death Valley."

I cough and suck down some slushy, forgetting it's supposed to be for Jake. "Confidential." There's no way I'm telling him I'm going to a regular old swamp in our own state. "You know, production and stuff."

Brad pays and we walk back outside. There's an even bigger swarm of people around the Jeep now and Dad's talking to a reporter who's probably supposed to be covering the race. Jake stands next to Dad, and I realize that he looks like the real thing: safari hat, khaki *Survivor Guy* button-down shirt, and cargo shorts. I know he got the hat at the Dollar Depot, but still, he looks like Survivor Guy's son.

"Well, good luck today," I say, and peel away from Brad. I try to run my fingers through my hair, but they get all tangled in the sticky parts.

And then I hear Dad say something about the Great Dismal Swamp and I know Brad hears him too. I shove through the crowd and climb back into the Jeep. I bang my head against the door frame, just once, just enough to dislodge the image of Brad sitting around his family room with popcorn and twenty of his closest buds watching me make an idiot of myself. Why didn't I tell everyone the truth to begin with? This is going to be a disaster.

By the time Jake and Dad finish signing autographs and taking pictures, I've eaten all the chocolate out of the trail mix and sucked down half of my orange fizz pizzazz. But I tell myself it's okay. For the next week, it's going to be grasshoppers and frog legs over a campfire for me anyway.

FIVE

Jake is snoring in the back seat. I pull out the General's book and look for anything more I can find about swamp survival.

"Is that Grandpa's book?" Dad asks. "You still have that?"

"Yep." There's a ton of information on mountain survival, which is ironic since Grandpa disappeared while climbing the Austrian Alps fifteen years ago.

"Greatest survivalist of all time," Dad says, grabbing the book and smelling it. "Maybe one day when you're old enough, we'll go look for him."

"In heaven?" I say, horrified.

"No, silly." Dad hands me the book back. "In Austria, of course."

"What are you talking about? He's dead. You had a funeral for him and everything."

Dad shakes his head. "Grandma had a funeral for him, but I think he's still out there somewhere." He looks mistily out the window. "Surviving."

I look over my shoulder to see if Jake's hearing any of this, but he's still sleeping, drooling all over the seat.

"Okay, Dad," I say, looking for a way to change the subject. I pull a map of Virginia from the glove box. "How far away are we?" The Great Dismal Swamp is not hard to find, a giant sprawling national park with a lake right in the middle.

Dad's ripping off a bite of beef jerky and driving with one hand now. "About two hours to go."

"That's it?" I say, because how exotic is that? I've driven farther for an archery meet.

"Yessir." He smacks his lips. "Practically in our backyard. Bite?" He thrusts the jerky in my face and I swat it away.

I look at all the regular people going on regular family vacations driving along the highway with us. Bikes tied to the backs, cargo pods fastened to the tops, back seats piled high with pillows and bags. Moms and dads sitting up front.

"So, this is the season finale?" I say. "Are you coming back home for a while after?"

Dad stops chewing and rests his beef jerky hand on my shoulder. "Ali, you know that your mom and I—"

"I know, I know." My stomach is getting all bounced up with the Jeep, swirling orange fizz pizzazz and chocolate candy bits.

"I want you to give Mom a break. This is hard for her too," Dad says.

"She doesn't let me do anything. You have no idea what it's like when you're not there." My face burns with shame, though, and I wonder if I should have let her hug me. It's just that lately, when she touches me or even gets near me, all I can think about is how she made Dad leave. And she had no right to do that.

"We'll always be a family, the four of us. I just might live in a different house."

Dad squeezes my shoulder and I knock his hand off. The look on his face is one of complete betrayal.

My stomach cramps. I might suffocate and die in this car if we don't get there soon.

"I need to go to the bathroom," I manage to say. My stomach is churning and grumbling and boiling.

Dad frowns. "Not many bathrooms around here. You'll have to wait for the next rest area."

I picture Dad's fans, all wearing cargo shorts and khaki button-downs with *Survivor Guy* binoculars hanging from their necks. Some of them even have the *Survivor Guy* compass and matching snakeskin pouch. It's not like mine though — I have the real thing. I feel for the bulge of it, safe in my pocket. I wonder if all those fans would be disappointed if Survivor Guy went to a plain old rest area when he needed to use the facilities on long car rides.

I vow to never drink another slushy in my life again. At ten a.m., anyway.

Dad looks at me. "You all right?"

Jake kicks the back of my seat, waking up and flailing himself upright.

I burp. "How long to the rest area?"

"Yeah, when's lunch?" asks Jake, letting out a gigantic moaning yawn.

I grab my stomach and look at my feet. Not at the

cars whizzing past us, or the trees waving at us with their leaves, or the rotting roadkill carcasses. I imagine the orange fizz pizzazz bubbling in my belly and the up-and-down bounce of the Jeep makes it bubble faster. I grab for the button to open the window, but it's not on the door or in the center console.

"I could go for some tasty barbecue," Jake says. "Some pulled pork smothered in greasy sauce—"

"How do you open the windows in this thing?" I ask, desperate for a gulp of real air, outside of the Jeep air, any air that I wasn't sharing with Jake or my dad and his beef jerky.

"It's manual," Jake says from the back, reaching over my head, his sweaty smell making me gag, to point out the handle on my door.

I crank it until my arm muscles are jelly, but it's still only open a baby crack. I crank some more, simultaneously wishing I'd actually used the weights in gym class and looking for an empty bag to stick my head into. The only one I find is the half-eaten bag of trail mix, and when I open it, the smell of peanuts and pretzels wafts out into the car.

I hear a thwack-splat against the windshield. "Did you see that?" Jake says, nearly leaping over the seats to point. "What was that, like an insect alien life form?"

I crank, crank, crank for my life.

"It was just a dragonfly," Dad says. "Big one. Must be getting closer to the swamp."

And that's all it takes. I lose the orange-fizz-pizzazz and chocolate-candy battle. All over the outside of Dad's Jeep.

SIX

We pour out of the Jeep gasping for air, as soon as Dad pulls over. "I told you not to invite her!" Jake yells.

I peel my socks off, because apparently I puked on myself as well. "I'm fine, if anyone cares."

Dad waves at us to be quiet. He's on his cell phone, pacing the side of the road. If Mom were here the Jeep would already be cleaned and disinfected. Jake and I stare at each other. "I'm not touching it," he says.

I give him my death glare and walk carefully to the back and open the hatch, trying not to brush anything against my contaminated clothes. Dad's duffel tumbles out, nearly killing me. I pull on Jake's bag, but it must weigh three thousand pounds. "What do you have in here?" I grunt. "A little help?" But Jake is busy pretending to gag into the ditch next to us.

I think I see movement inside an abandoned old gas station beyond the ditch, and when I look closer, I see a silhouette of a person through the broken screen door. I yelp, nearly stumbling back into the road, just as Jake's bag manages to unwedge itself and slide out of the car. I roll away from it Indiana Jones style.

"You all need any help?" Silhouette says from behind the screen, and I bounce back onto my feet.

There's pizzazz on my arm now. I am frozen. Silhouette could be a roadside serial killer and I'd be completely defenseless.

The screen door opens and out shuffles a little old lady in a housedress, a puff of some sort of animal under her arm. "You out of gas? Closest station is about twenty miles west of here."

The orange puff of fur barks hysterically and she stuffs him under her sweater. It must be nearly one hundred degrees, and she's wearing a sweater fit for the arctic tundra.

"So this is what we're going to do," Dad says, striding up to us, out of breath, oblivious to the sweater lady standing there. "We're taking a boat from the canal to Lake Drummond, where the production crew found a nice dry place to—" Dad notices the lady. "Hello." He pockets his phone and looks from the dilapidated gas station to our car to me.

"You headed to the swamp?" Sweater Lady asks, a look on her face like shock mixed together with horror.

"Yes, ma'am. Survivor Guy here." Dad points to himself.

Sweater Lady looks annoyed.

"Outdoor Central? Channel 62 on Lox Cable, 88 on satellite?" Dad tries, his chest deflating as he realizes his celebrity has not made it to this abandoned gas station. "Every Sunday at eight p.m.?"

"Ain't no one in his right mind in the swamp this time of year." She swats a mosquito away from Orange Puffball. "You got bug nets?"

Dad clears his throat, and I can tell the only kind of nets he has are the ones hanging bedraggled from the animal traps.

"Where you all from?" she says, talking to me all of a sudden.

"Northern Virginia," I say, flapping a swarm of gnats from my ears.

"Ever heard of yellow flies?" she asks.

"*Homarus americanus*? Yes, yes I have," Dad says, and I look at him because *Homarus americanus* is the scientific name for lobster.

"Does Dad have any bug nets?" I say to Jake, but he's collecting rocks from the side of the road like a three-year-old. "Dad? We have nets, right?"

Dad jostles me around by my shoulders like I have nothing to worry about, until he gets a real good whiff of me and backs away. Sweater Lady grabs my wrist and drags me toward the abandoned building. "You need to get cleaned up." I try to pull free but her grip is strong and Dad waves me on as he answers his phone again.

"Jake?" I try, desperate for anyone to join us inside, wishing that Mom was here, and wondering how many dead bodies I'll have to climb over to get to the bathroom.

"Dad?" I say, and then I yank my arm away. "I'm not supposed to go anywhere with strangers." Shouldn't my dad know that? Has he spent too many years in the wild?

"I'm no stranger," the old lady says. "Name's Betsy Sue. I've been living outside of this swamp for fifty years. Raised six kids and a miniature pony in these parts."

It's about three hundred fifty degrees inside the building. "You live here?" I ask before I can stop myself. There are towers of bowls and baking sheets, mounds of whisks, spoons, and empty pink boxes, and an avalanche of books in the corner.

"Does it look like I live here?" she says, leading me toward the back.

I can't see Dad or Jake through the screen door anymore and I panic, but then the cool air in the back room makes me want to melt into the armchair looking out onto the yard. It's clean and homey. I search for signs of a thousand cats or more piles of hoarded junk, but there's nothing out of the ordinary. Orange Puff slips out of Betsy Sue's arms and settles into the tiny doggie couch beneath the bay window.

"Bathroom's over there." She points with a craggly finger to an open door.

As soon as I close it behind me, I realize I don't have any clothes to change into. I hold my breath as I pull off my shirt, and try to splash-clean it in the sink without getting the entire thing wet. I attempt to wash my hair with the hand soap and call to Jake telepathically to bring my bag inside, knowing it's no use. He's probably still collecting rocks and wouldn't hear me if I called him with a bullhorn.

There's a knock. "Someone's in here!" I call.

"I know that, you loony bin," Betsy Sue says. "Thought you'd be needing this."

I crack the door open and she thrusts a shirt at me. Puffball is at her feet and barks at me all over again. "Will you cut that out!" she yells, and then nearly shuts the door on my fingers.

I shake out the shirt and pull it over my head. It's white with dark pink writing: SWEET TREAT BAKE SHOP, NOT EVERYTHING'S DISMAL IN THE GREAT DISMAL SWAMP. It's tight around my belly and all loose and ballooned where my chest should go. I will never eat another piece of chocolate again. I suck in my gut and take a second look at myself. I wring out my hair once more, give it a sniff test, and head out of the bathroom.

Betsy Sue is hovering over her coffee table, a smattering of outdoor gear spread out before her. She lifts a hat, hooded with nets and zippers, and hands it to me. "No one in their right mind goes in the swamp this time of year," she warns. "Take this and maybe you'll be the only one to survive."

If Harper was with me, we'd be on the floor laughing, because there is no way I am wearing that, especially if there's a camera involved. It looks like something you'd need when the plague hit or if you were a killer-bee keeper. Brad Garrison watches *Survivor Guy*. That helmet will never touch my head.

"Take it," she says, pushing it into my chest. I do as she says, but promise nothing.

"My boy Robbie-Jay used it every day. He really loved the swamp, you know. Right up until the end." Betsy Sue looks wistful. "Actually, I think he was wearing it that last day."

"Last day? What last day?" I ask, holding the helmet away from me.

"Don't worry about returning that shirt," Betsy Sue says.

I shake my head. "I shouldn't take this." I hand her the helmet back. "It's special to you."

She cackles. "He deserved it." She picks Puffball off the floor and strokes his fur. "Ever heard the saying 'you don't poke a sleeping bear'?"

"There are bears in the swamp?" I ask.

"Of course. Snakes, bears, alligators, yellow flies." She swats the air even though nothing is there.

I pull at my shirt, wondering if I should call Mom. If I told her about all the dangerous predators I'm about to face, not to mention the fact that I was lured into a strange lady's house without a chaperone, she'd be on the next plane to get me.

"Sounds like your daddy's used to those kinds of things though." Puffball is snuggling in her arms now. "And he won't be the first. Legend has it whole flocks of people survived in the swamp for years, generations even. People escaping slavery, runaways, ghosts."

"Ghosts?" I say, startled. Where is Dad taking me?

We pass through the mess in the front room and Betsy Sue rattles off a thousand terrifying facts about yellow flies and how they swarm and how to outrun them and what to do if they catch you.

I'm relieved, for once in my life, to see Jake staring at me through the screen door. "Get a move on!" he says. "Dad already had to push back production three hours."

I see Dad at the Jeep, throwing a pail of water on the spot where I lost my breakfast.

"Thank you," I tell Betsy Sue. I try and pat her little dog, but his teeth, which are giant compared to the rest of his body, come out of nowhere and snap at my fingers.

"What is that?" Jake asks, pointing at my helmet.

I run for the Jeep. "Just get in the car!"

Jake slides in behind me, and as soon as the doors are closed, we're off.

"Hope that hat brings more luck to you than it did to my Robbie-Jay!" Betsy Sue calls after us.

Dad beeps the horn and we wave.

"Do you know the swamp is filled with ghosts?" I ask.

"FACT!" Dad says. "There is no such thing as ghosts."

"It smells like puke in here, can we just get there?" Jake moans from the back.

"Baby," I call him.

"Scaredy-pants," he says.

Dad opens all the windows and I drop the helmet on the floor and check my cell phone. No service. I lean back, letting the hot, humid air tumble over me. Great Dismal Swamp, here I come.

SEVEN

Dad pulls off the gravel road next to the sign that says INTERIOR DITCH, GREAT DISMAL SWAMP, VISIT AT YOUR OWN RISK. We bump to a stop and twenty or thirty horseflies immediately land on the Jeep. I put a lot of effort into rolling up my window. Jake bursts out laughing and I stare at the helmet at my feet. Perhaps I will use it after all. Off camera, anyway.

Dad's already out of the car, not scared of anything, especially a tiny little black fly. "After you," I tell Jake, wondering how I got stuck doing the Dismal Swamp when Jake's first *Survivor Guy* trip was to a deserted Caribbean island.

Dad knocks on my window and the flies disperse

in a black cloud. He waves for me to come out. There are three people dressed in safari gear grinning next to him, one behind a giant camera and another carrying a pole with a fuzzy top.

"Rick, Bianca, and Wes," Jake introduces them. "The producer, lead camera, and audio."

"I thought Dad was the cameraman," I say.

Dad taps on my window again. "Come on out," he mouths.

I open the door, suddenly very aware I'm the only one not in survivalist gear. Even Jake has his hiking boots on. When did he change into those? I flip-flop next to my dad, tugging my shirt. "Is that on?" I say to the camera.

"It's always on, honey," Dad answers.

"What happened to the tiny camera that fits in your shirt pocket?" I ask. "The one with a raccoon bite?"

"We have it." Dad swats at a fly. "It doesn't work, but we still use it in shots."

Bianca extends a hand. I shake it, trying to avoid colliding my face with the piece of equipment on her shoulder.

"Is there going to be a charger at camp?" Jake asks, looking at his phone.

I laugh because any serious survivalist knows there's no electricity in the middle of the wild. But if we were having an emergency, we could read chapter fifteen in Grandpa's book: "Wilderness Wind Power and You."

"Of course," Dad replies, walking down a short path.

"Seriously?" I say.

"Just a few gas generators. For the equipment."

The boat launch comes into view and it's abuzz with people wearing matching *Survivor Guy* shirts and visors, carrying trunks and cases. One guy walks past me with a cappuccino machine. "How much equipment, Dad?"

There are several small boats in the water, already loaded up with *Survivor Guy* gear, bags and tubs and metal containers. I see a giant pot in one of the boats, too clean and sparkly to have ever been cooked over a fire.

"Dad?"

Some woman with a CREW shirt passes by with

our luggage and starts tossing it into a boat next to a canoe. I quick-grab the hiking boots tied to the top of my bag and swap out my flip-flops, stuffing Grandpa's book in too, under my clothes for safekeeping.

Jake climbs into the canoe, rocking it back and forth and pretend-screaming, waving his hands in the air, looking like a complete moron. Bianca stares at him, her camera to her side. A row of fishermen standing along the water give up and pull their lines out. They sit on their coolers because all the benches are taken up by production stuff.

"Ali-Gator!" Dad calls to me, and half the crew freezes. Dad smiles. "No. This little alligator. Get it? Ali-Gator?" While Dad laughs at his own joke, everyone relaxes, all eyes on me and my too-tight bakery T-shirt. And then Dad does this "zip-a-dee-doo-dah" whistle and everyone unfreezes and whistles "zip-a-dee-ay" back. "Time to get in the boats," he says.

The crew swarms the bank of the canal. Bag lady throws the last of our stuff into the boat next to us and I have to squeeze through a throng of people wearing *Survivor Guy* visors to reach Dad. He's already in the canoe. He extends his hand, and someone lifts me from behind and deposits me next to Jake. I hear crackling walkie-talkies, boat motors sputtering. I whirl around, remembering my helmet. It's on the luggage boat, right on top in case I need it. I have a five-second freak-out as a fly lands on me, but I remain calm on the outside. The camera is pointed directly at me.

Jake stands up in the boat, nearly tipping us over, and I get a close-up of the water. It's chocolate brown, like it's straight out of Willy Wonka's factory. But when I dip my hand in, it drips clean and clear from my fingers.

I take the middle plank seat as Jake grabs an oar and sits up front. Dad takes the seat behind me and helps Jake paddle, steering the boat in the right direction. The canoe is tippy and I'm uncomfortable. Even with all my extra padding, my butt goes numb within three seconds.

"Are there life preservers on this boat?" I ask.

"Hope you don't get seasick," Jake says over his shoulder.

Rick, the production guy, revs the engine of the boat behind us and flies away from the shore, Bianca and Wes kneeling inside. They take some shots in front of us and then to the right, Rick telling us to face forward like we're George Washington seeing the swamp for the first time. That reminds me of school and sixth-grade graduation—and Harper, who probably still hates me. She never even responded to my text.

I look over my shoulder, and the Jeep and the rest of the crew are tiny ants behind us. I have another secret freak-out because I'll be sleeping in a shelter made of leaves and twigs and spiderwebs, eating moss for breakfast, and taking pee breaks in the bear- and bug-infested woods.

And there's no turning back.

EIGHT

When the narrow Interior Ditch waterway dumps us into Lake Drummond, it's like coming out of the dense jungle and into the wide open. The lake is so huge ahead of us, all I can see is water for miles. Dad nudges me. "If you ever wonder why I do what I do . . ." He rests his paddle on his lap and spreads his arms out like all of this belongs to him.

I try to take everything in. The dark chocolate water, the butterflies, the giant trees sprouting right out of the lake, their roots exposed like a fish obstacle course.

"Archery matches are pretty cool too," I say, because Harper's dad goes to every single one, even though she's terrible.

Dad doesn't hear me, his eyes closed, his whole face lit by the sun. My stomach growls, apparently fully recovered from the earlier trauma and ready for a snack. Jake shoots me a look, then goes back to paddling. Camera-lady Bianca is loving my dad sitting there in complete Survivor Guy bliss. The camera boat is staying right beside us, the fumes from the motor making me dizzy on top of my lightheadedness from lack of food.

"We'll need some water shots." Rick calls. "Let's stop here."

Dad stands up and pulls open a trunk behind him. It's not filled with life preservers like I had thought, but with long wading overalls. He pulls out three and hands Jake and me each a pair. "Dad?" I say.

"Go ahead and pull the plug when you're ready," Rick yells across the water.

"What plug?" I ask.

"How long do we have to walk?" Jake says, scanning the lake. "I don't see the camp."

"We're getting in the lake?"

Rick spins the camera boat around so Bianca's camera is in my face, and the audio guy positions his boom mic to hover directly over my head. I swat them away, along with the dozen or so little black flies that discover us as soon as our boat floats to a stop.

"Just for a bit, sweetie," Dad says, like we're stopping for milkshakes or something. "This episode is called 'When Fishing with the Family Goes Bad.' We just need to set things up."

"There are alligators in swamps!" I shriek, and the crew snickers. "There are!" I read about them in chapter three, "Southern Swamps and How Not to Get Eaten by a Predator," in the General's book.

Dad holds on to my shoulder for balance as he puts his overalls on. "FACT! We're still too far north for alligators. You think I'd put you in an alligator-infested lake?"

"For the record, it was supposed to be called 'When Father-Son Fishing Goes Bad,'" Jake adds. He sits on the edge of the boat, yanks a plug out of the floor, and flings himself into the water, nearly capsizing us. Water bubbles up from the small hole and I rush into my own waders, checking to make sure my compass is tucked safely in my pocket. Jake stands up, as surprised as I am to find the lake is only about four feet deep here. Not enough water to seep over his overalls, but plenty for a hungry alligator to hide in, if you ask me. I'm sweating, pulling up my waders, but they're not going on easy like they are for everyone else.

Dad steps into the lake like a normal human being, one leg at a time, and then he approaches the camera. He's out of breath all of a sudden, like he's just finished a triathlon. "Lake Drummond," he says into the lens. "One of two natural freshwater lakes in Virginia. A day out fishing with the family, when disaster strikes."

Bianca swings her camera in my direction and I realize I'm alone on the boat. Where is Rick? And then I see him catching up to Jake a few feet away, wearing his own set of waders. I tug at my overalls, not about to be left out in the middle of a swampy lake by myself. I nearly have a hysterical fit when something cold and slithery touches my arm. The canoe sways dangerously and I see it's only the metal handle of the oar. I stare at Dad.

He's talking into the camera again. "Serenity for miles and miles." He moves his arm over the water, letting some sprinkle through his fingers. "Just goes to show that danger can lurk anywhere."

"Dad?" I say. "Some help?"

". . . two-mile walk to shore with only enough water packed for a day trip and no food . . ."

I manage to get my foot stuck sideways in my wader. The puddle on the floor of the boat has swelled to a little pool. "Dad!"

I try waving to get Jake's attention, but he's giggling with Rick about something. When did they get to be such good friends? I look down to find the pool up to my ankles now. "This boat is sinking!"

I stand to yank up my overalls and the boat tips again, so I collapse back to the floor, grabbing the sides for dear life, splashing swamp water into my face. I stand again slowly and swing a leg over the side, reaching in vain for some solid ground, the boat threatening to flip. I shimmy closer to the side of the boat, but it's not enough. "Dad?" The boat is half filled with swamp now and I feel the cool water against the back of my waders. "Jake?"

I try to hop in like my dad, but it's not working, so I slide into the water on my belly, feet first, holding on to one of the seats for leverage. But the bottom of the lake is too far, so I'm left dangling, praying the camera is still focused on Dad. I hear splashing behind me. "Ali!" Dad calls.

I'm fully in the water now, my feet on the soft peat floor of the swamp. Dad grabs me and wraps me in a hug. I want to yell at him for not rescuing me. I mean, is this how the rest of the week is going to go? Instead, I squeeze him back and we watch the canoe submerge into the chocolate darkness.

"Fabulous father-daughter moment. Just fabulous!" Rick says, and I'm beginning to dislike the guy.

Jake appears beside us. "We might need this for shelter." He lifts the nose of the canoe back out of the water, checking over his shoulder to make sure the camera is still rolling. "Night is about to fall."

I look at the sky. Yeah, in about four hours. But Dad must think it's a good idea too because they are both inching the sunken boat across the lake. Bianca and her camera are in the water now with Wes close by in the boat, his boom mic extended over the lake on a long pole. Bianca wades up to me with Rick, trying to keep their equipment dry. "Mind talking about the boat accident into the camera?" Bianca says, and before I can respond, I see the little red light ping on and Rick flashes me a thumbs-up sign.

"Uh, well, it wasn't really an accident, right? Jake

pulled the plug and the boat started filling up with water. I tried getting out, but it was really hard with these on." I snap a strap of my overalls. They're still staring at me so I say, "The end."

"Uh, great. Thanks." Bianca looks at Rick and I can tell it's not exactly the accident report they're looking for. They drift off toward their boat.

Behind them the rest of the crew heaves the canoe up out of the lake and pours all the water out of it. Three of the guys haul it onto their heads and start marching toward a little column of smoke drifting into the sky on the shore.

Jake joins me and Dad and we start our trek in the same direction, my legs burning from the effort of moving through the water after only a few strides. Rick, Bianca, and Wes glide along next to us in the safety of their boat.

My waders weigh three thousand pounds. "Are we almost there?" I ask. I hear Wes snicker. They're probably going to make me look like this scaredy-baby that doesn't want to break a nail. I look at my hands and realize that, even though I've never had a manicure before, if given the choice between slogging through alligator waters in the middle of a swamp or getting a manicure, I'd have to go with getting my nails done. Guess I'm more like Mom in that way.

"Ouch!" Jake cradles his arm. "Something jumped out of the water and bit me."

Bianca is there first, getting Jake's agony on tape.

"Am I bleeding? That's blood, right?"

Dad lunges through the water. "Swamp muskie."

"It just leaped up and bit me," Jake says into the camera. "His teeth were like five inches long."

Swamp muskie? I pull my arms out of the water. We're walking again, Jake asking about rabies and Lyme disease and Dad talking about swamp muskies into the camera. I shuffle faster, cringing each time my feet sink into the peat, hoping I don't stir up anything else. "I'm not dinner," I whisper toward the water. Although I could use some myself.

"What's that, Ali-Gator?"

Everyone spins around and the crew halts. "Ali-Gator," Dad says, pointing to me. "My little alligator."

Rick shakes his head from his boat. "Say aye if Ali-Gator needs a new nickname."

"Aye!" everyone says.

NINE

After what feels like an hour of walking through the thick water in the beating-down sun, the column of smoke we're slogging toward looks no closer. My legs are dead weight, and my arms are tingly from holding them out of reach of the swamp muskies. And if one more creature bumps against my waders, I will have a total freak-out right here in the middle of Lake Drummond.

"Swamp muskies jump, you know," Jake says, still holding his arm delicately.

"How many people work here?" I ask, counting one camera lady, a producer, a sound guy, a woman driving the luggage boat, and three guys heaving the canoe across the lake over their heads. That's seven people. Not exactly one guy, one camera, and miles and miles of unforgiving wilderness.

"Takes a lot of people to make a successful TV show," Dad says.

"But I thought it was just you and a camera."

Dad looks at me. "That's just our show's slogan. You know that."

"No, I didn't," I say, because isn't the whole point of this show for him to teach the people of the world how to save themselves if they ever have to survive in the wild alone?

"Oh, sweetheart." He gives me a sideways hug.

"Alison never pays attention to anything," Jake says.

"Not true!" I say, because there are a ton of things I pay attention to. Like the suffocating heat and humidity of this place. And the gathering clouds above us. Great. All we need is a rainstorm.

"What's my girlfriend's name?" Jake says.

"You have a girlfriend?"

He shakes his head, but I ignore him. How am I supposed to keep up with all the details of his social life?

The guys carrying the canoe are so far ahead of us, all I can see is the up-and-down bob of the boat on their heads. It's only us back here still in the middle of the lake. Dad, Jake, and me. And the camera boat, of course. I want to climb in and collapse on the bottom of it with a bag of trail mix. That's right. I'm so hungry, I'd eat a bag of trail mix. And this time I'd eat all the healthy junk too.

"You are forlorn," Rick says from the comfort of the boat. "Hopeless. Will you make it? Is there any chance of rescue in this unforgiving wilderness?"

I don't have to act. I am the combination of forlornity and hopelessness all bundled into one. Dad and Jake are splashing each other and seeing who can run the farthest without falling in the water.

"You are stranded in the middle of the Great Dismal Swamp, people!" Rick says.

Dad and Jake straighten. I try to catch up, but my feet are like cinder blocks. Dad turns to the camera, all of a sudden serious and foreboding. He cups a handful of water. "Some say these waters are healing waters. Something my son Jake here will soon find out." Dad pours some over Jake's muskie bite, which looks more like a mosquito bite to me. He gently holds Jake's arm and Jake winces. Since when did he become such a great actor? Is this entire show one big act?

"Dad," I say, impatient. "How much longer until we're out of this lake?" Not like I'm particularly looking forward to arriving on the banks of this nasty swamp, because then what? We pitch a tent out of leaves and call it a night?

"Ow!" Producer guy stands up wildly in the boat. "I just got bit." He swats around his head. "There's another one. Ouch!" He crouches over, still trying to bat away whatever is biting him. "They're swarming me!" Bianca is standing now too, dropping her camera, the boat tipping and swaying.

Yellow flies. I jog clumsily through the water. Where's that helmet? But it's long gone to shore on the luggage boat. "You've got to start moving," I say. "Six to seven miles per hour!" I quote Betsy Sue. "Go, go!"

The boat motor comes to life and they circle around us. Dad and Jake are still standing there and I splash past them. "Run!" I say. "Yellow flies!"

Jake laughs. "I hope you got that, Bianca," he calls.

And that's when I feel the first bite. No buzzing, no warning, just a stinging pain in my shoulder. And then another one on my back. I am running as fast as I can, smacking flies from my arms and shoulders, dousing my head with water. I trip, feel cold swamp fill my waders, and push myself off the bottom with my hand, dunking my entire body.

Dad runs past, arms waving. "Grab onto me!" He extends his hand for me to take, but I miss it and he keeps running, leaving me there.

I stand up, the relief of the cool water already gone, and cringe at the sight of my arms and the swollen bites. "Jake!" I call behind me. "Don't just stand there! You have to run." I can actually see the swarm of flies circling him. It's like getting out of there hadn't occurred to him, because as soon as I suggest it, he bolts in my direction. And all I can think is, his swarm of flies will be looking for fresh blood. I take off the same way Dad went, but Jake passes me easily.

"Wait for me!" I yell, but neither Jake nor Dad turns around. It's every man for himself out here. "Dad!"

I fall again, this time getting a mouthful of swamp water, my waders fully flooded. They must weigh three tons now, and I start to wonder how I'll ever get out of this lake. I hear a boat and I stand up to see Dad and Jake waving at it hysterically. But the boat comes to me first. It has the *Survivor Guy* logo on the side, but the driver is new. And a kid.

"Get in," he says.

"How old are you?" I ask, trying to hop in the boat without flipping it over.

"Old enough," he replies, even though he looks barely older than me. "I'm Adam, the summer intern."

He hauls me onto the boat and helps me struggle out of my waders. I check to make sure my compass is still in my pocket, and then collapse onto the floor.

We take off, the wind feeling wonderful against my throbbing skin.

TEN

My skin is on fire by the time we step onto shore.

"This way," Adam says, pulling my elbow, leading me past the rest of the boats already tied up.

"What about my dad?" I look over my shoulder to scan the lake, because everyone is out now except for Dad and Jake. I get distracted by the flies. There are more. Hundreds more. Swarms of them by the trees.

"How are we going to sleep outside like this?" I ask. "We'll get eaten alive."

"Outside?" Adam looks toward the trees and snorts. "Ha! That's hilarious."

My arms are itchy and bulgy with bites, and for once I wish Mom was here. She has a superhero skin-care cream for every occasion. I don't want to look like a monster my first time on TV.

"Why is that so hilarious?"

Rick and Bianca burst through the trees. "Run, Ali!" they say. "Over here!"

And I do, because what nutjob would stand around in an insect- and snake-infested swamp when two grownups tell you to run like your life depends on it? Not this nutjob. I run, even though my legs are soggy from the trek through the lake, leaping over knee-high weeds, tripping over puddles of swamp until I reach the safety of the trees.

"Good job," Rick says, jiggling me and patting me on the back. "Great, just great. Could really see the fear. You ever been on camera before?"

I look back at Adam and he's bent over, laughing.

"Get some footage of them coming in," Rick tells Bianca, waving toward Jake and my dad puttering in on another boat. "Son, take Ali to the dining tent and touch base with the animal trainer," he tells Adam.

I stand straighter. "No thanks, I'll just wait for my dad."

"Schedule's tight." Rick squeezes my shoulder. "Go get some dinner."

Adam walks right past me, and Rick gives me a push to follow. I step over roots and rocks, watching for spiderwebs, following Adam. Then I come into a clearing. A giant clearing in the middle of the Great Dismal Swamp with flowers and mowed grass and walking bridges over a little canal of rich brown water. Beyond the walking bridges is an old brick cottage with a big screened-in porch, a mammoth camping trailer, a bunch of tents, a circle of smaller trailers, and dozens of people whizzing around in camouflage-colored golf carts. I freeze. This is not *Survivor Guy*. This is a circus.

"Wait," Adam says, glancing back at me. "You've never been on set before?"

I feel red-hot-lobster face creeping up my neck. "Sure, like a million times."

"Wow. A million." He smirks. "That's sure a lot."

There must be more than twenty or thirty people walking around, carrying fishing nets and piles of wood and pushing rolling crates full of props. Flopped over the side of one is a plastic bat wing, painted swirly black and gray. The big bat-attack scene in the Rocky Mountain cave episode? Was that just a prop?

"What did you think?" Adam says. "That your dad was a real survivor guy?"

Yes. I thought he was a man with a camera and miles and miles of unforgiving wilderness. It's what the deep-voiced narrator says at the start of each episode. And why wouldn't I believe that? Adam nudges me toward one of the tents and I feel a familiar fire in my belly. The one that always starts up when the nonbelievers in school tell me my dad's a big fake.

"He fended off a school of man-eating sharks when he was thirteen, you know." I cross my arms, trying not to scratch.

"Man-eating, huh?" Adam flaps open the door to the tent, the scents of fresh bread and fried chicken and bug spray wafting out. "I never said it's not a good show." He disappears inside and I check once more to see if Dad and Jake are back on shore yet, then follow.

There are more people in here, heaping fried chicken and buttered rolls onto their plates. There's a meat carver. An actual guy wearing a fancy white uniform slicing off succulent pieces of ham. "How long has everyone worked here?" I ask Adam, who's taking an extra long time choosing a piece of fried chicken goodness. My stomach growls.

He licks his fingers and picks up his tray. "What do you mean? Um, like, forever I guess."

"Never mind, how would you know, anyway?" It's obvious I'm not going to be friends with this kid. "You're just an intern."

He tongs a butter roll. "Whoa. Sensing some hostility here. Don't get mad at *me* about all this." He plops the bread onto my plate. "Wabam."

My belly is burning hotter and hotter as I take in the dining tent, because there are exactly zero grasshoppers or swamp muskies on the menu. It's a full-on food paradise here, and it's like I'm the only one who didn't know. I fork a piece of chicken, skip the green beans even though they're swimming in butter, and sit at the nearest empty table. I wish there was a curtain I could just disappear behind and blot out the rest of the world. But there's Adam, right behind me.

"I'm fourteen, by the way. Going to high school next year." He slides into the chair across from me.

"What are you, like, ten or eleven? Why haven't you been on set before?"

"Twelve, thank you very much." I pick up a piece of greasy chicken. "And I'm too busy with archery to come on set all the time like some people. I get most-improved player every year. My team can't survive without me."

"Wow, that sounds like a lot of responsibility." Is he snickering? I drop my drumstick, ready to tell him a thing or two about archery responsibility, when a guy sits down at the table with us.

"This is Samuel. Your dad's stunt double." Adam points to him. "This is the guy that sleeps outside."

"For part of the night, at least," Samuel says, scratching his own arms swollen with yellow fly bites.

I do my best impression of a smile and pick the fried part off my chicken. I thought I'd be eating beetles and small rodents cooked over a fire. Surviving in the wild is supposed to mean sacrifice. Grandpa once survived three nights in a crevasse in the middle of a glacier with only a bag of almonds. Across the tent, I see a soft-serve ice cream station and bowls of candy toppings. A little bit of sacrifice, at least.

And then I hear the "zip-a-dee-doo-dah" whistle,

and Jake and my dad walk in, Dad rubbing his belly with one hand and waving to the crew with the other. "Evening, folks!" Jake already has a plate and is digging into a vat of baked beans.

Everyone stands up, whistling "zip-a-dee-ay" back to Dad. Even Adam. Samuel shoots up from the table and greets Dad with a handshake and a rough swat on his shoulder like they're old college buddies. The kitchen staff hustles together a plate and delivers it to Dad, who heads toward me, shaking hands and fist-bumping all the way.

"Everyone's excited about the news," Adam whispers.

"What news?"

Dad sits next to me, pounding the table with a fist. "Episode seventy-five, here we come!"

Adam is staring at me, eyebrows raised. I take another bite, ignoring him.

"Samuel." Dad nods to his stunt double. "We have quite a doozy set up for after dinner. How do you feel about snakes?"

Jake stumbles over to the table, his arms and face puffed and seepy with bites.

"Jake!" I say. "How many bites do you have?"

Adam and Samuel lean away from him, as he sits and looks at me with glassy eyes. "This steak looks delicious."

"That's fried chicken, dude," Adam says.

"Are you feeling okay?" I ask.

Dad touches Jake's head. "He's fine. Just a few bites."

Adam pulls back Jake's shirt sleeve. "Some of these are hives."

Jake takes a giant forkful of baked beans from his plate, staring at it. "Actually, I think maybe—"

And then he passes out cold on the floor.

ELEVEN

Before I know what's happening, Adam lunges across the table and jabs Jake in the thigh with an EpiPen. I stand up, my chair thumping to the dirt floor, helpless. Dad bolts out of the tent, a chicken thigh still in his hand.

One of the kitchen staff sprints over with an open bottle of glass cleaner and puts it under Jake's nose, trying to wake him up, splashing his shirt, the stench of ammonia reaching all the way to me. Adam is going through all the proper survival first-aid procedures I've read about and know by heart. Checking for a pulse, stabilizing his neck. And I just stand there, stupid.

Jake opens his eyes and tries to sit up, shivering in the ninety-degree heat.

"Allergic reaction," Adam says to him. "You'll be okay."

Dad jogs back into the tent with a blond lady carrying a backpack with a red cross on it, and the crowd around my brother clears a path. "Who had an EpiPen?" she says. "Nice job."

Jake is sweating and shivering and scratching his arms and neck. The woman pulls his hands away and checks his vitals while Dad paces behind them. I pull at my shirt and redo my ponytail, feeling like everyone's looking at me, wondering why the daughter of a famed survivalist didn't know what to do when her own brother keeled over.

Adam helps heave Jake to his feet and the woman and Dad guide him toward the exit. Even his legs are covered in hives, and I wonder if this means we're going home. And I hope Harper doesn't ever ask me about how I got to spend two hours on the *Survivor Guy* set, because then I might have to tell her the truth about all of Dad's lies. She'll think we're just a big family of liars.

"Hornets," Adam says to everyone still standing

around. "I'm allergic to hornets. Always have an Epi-Pen or two."

The medical bag hangs open on one of the chairs, so I zip it up and sling it over my back, jogging to catch up to Dad and Jake. I follow them outside, checking for yellow flies over my shoulder, flapping my hands over my head just in case of an attack, when a little girl comes racing out of one of the other tents. "George!" she squeals, rocketing herself into Dad's arms.

Dad lets go of Jake and the medical lady barely catches him. I hurry to his side and grab him, staring at the little girl with Dad. He's flipping around pretending he doesn't see her even though she's hanging off his elbow. "Isabel? Isabel? Where'd she go?" He used to do the same thing to me.

"I'm here! I'm here!" she screams, grabbing Dad's cheeks and squeezing them into a fish face.

The woman peers around Jake. "I'm Claire. I'm the medic on set."

I peel my eyes off the scene behind me and shake her extended hand. Jake coughs and stumbles. "Is he going to be okay?" I ask.

Claire pats him on the back. "A little rest and

epinephrine will do him just fine. I take it you're Alison?"

I nod my head, and Dad gallops past us into the tent, Isabel hanging on to his neck by her spindly arms.

"Be careful with that child!" Claire yells. "He's a silly man." She shakes her head. "Always playing. Never serious." It's exactly what Mom says. Even in the middle of a fight, he'll make a joke or give her a death-grip-tickle to the knee. She hates that. "It's why everyone loves him so much."

I cough. "Right, yes, exactly why."

Inside the tent is a makeshift hospital. There are two beds and an IV pole and some kind of monitor on wheels. There's another room in the back, its canvas door flapped open to reveal rolls of bandages, a pair of crutches, and other medical stuff. Dad is leaned over one bed, catching his breath. The little girl runs up to me, nearly pirouetting into a basket of gauze.

"I'm Isabel. I'm going to kindergarten."

Claire and I heave Jake onto the other bed. "Hi."

Isabel grabs my hand. "This is where I sleep." There's a third room, divided by a wall of towels clipped to the top of the tent. Princess and emoji and tie-dye. I peek inside. It's the medic's bedroom. Isabel pulls a hammock hanging between two of the tent poles and swings it wildly. "But we're going home soon so we can sign me up for kindergarten where there will be kids my own age. And our house will have a giant big-kid bed with a closet and also a window. And there won't even be any wild animals. Just normal walls and beds and stuff."

"I think you have a new friend." Dad laughs behind me. "She must be able to tell how much you love kids."

Is he joking? I like kids about as much as I like veggie burgers. Not at all. I rub my now-sticky hand on my shorts.

"Want to try? You're kind of"—she puffs her cheeks out and pops them with a finger—"but I won't be mad if you break it." Isabel offers me her hammock, but I am open-mouthed offended at her insinuation. Who does this girl think she is?

Jake moans from his bed. "My steak," he says. "I didn't get to finish it." And I know he'll be just fine. If ever there's a time when Jake's not hungry, that's when you call for the medevac helicopter.

A girl wearing a *Survivor Guy* cap pokes her head

into the tent. "Animal encounter at seven, George. Don't forget." And then she swings back around, revealing a mesh bag hanging over her shoulder.

"Are those snakes?" I ask.

"Come on, my little alligators," Dad says. "Let's let Jake get some sleep."

Alligators? As in plural? I turn around and find Isabel koala-beared to Dad's leg. He used to hate it when I did that. It reminded him of an unfortunate encounter with a lemur in Madagascar.

"Don't lose her, Georgie!" Claire calls, and Isabel squeals as Dad shakes her off his leg.

I know I shouldn't care, because she's a little kid and lives in a tent, and I guess she's cute, with her pudgy cheeks and pigtails. But all I can think is that there's room for only one alligator in this swamp.

TWELVE

Dad leads us to a golf cart with off-roading tires by a stack of heavy-duty containers. "What are those?" I'm about to sit down when Isabel squeezes past me and climbs into the seat next to Dad.

"Gas. For the generators."

I push in, but half my butt is hanging out of the cart. I push harder.

"Ow!" Isabel rubs her shoulder. "Can I sit on your lap?" And before I can say absolutely not, she hops right on me, half wringing my neck.

"Crew gets grumpy without hot showers and running water," Dad says, ignoring the fact that I've just been almost asphyxiated by a four-year-old. He hits the gas pedal and for a moment the breeze gives some relief from the heat. Then my hair starts sticking to my face and neck.

"My new house will have a bathtub," Isabel pipes up.

"Dad?" I say. "I didn't realize you had such a big crew."

"Yeah, I tried going solo for about two episodes and then got bit by a rattler and had to walk seven miles to find help." He shakes his head. "Had to make a tourniquet out of my underwear."

Isabel snorts. "You said underwear."

"Really? Only two episodes? Does Mom know?"

"Sure." Dad's driving way too fast on this tiny grassy island in the middle of the swamp. He hits a rock and I swear we're going to tip, but somehow the golf cart manages to right itself and slam back down onto four wheels. "She'd have never let you come here otherwise."

"Why didn't anyone tell me?" I say. Isabel's trying to braid my ponytail, her sweaty arms in my face, and I pull her away.

"Guess I thought you knew," Dad says, parking in front of a brown and black camper that looks like it belongs to a mega-millionaire celebrity. And then I remember my dad is the celebrity. Maybe not a mega-millionaire, but a celebrity.

"Quick stop," he says.

Isabel scrambles out and races to the trailer. "I'm the rotten egg!"

Dad laughs. "The last person is the rotten egg. You don't want to be the rotten egg."

He pats me on the back like "isn't she the cutest?" but all I can think is something sure smells rotten to me.

Dad turns off the golf cart and we follow Isabel inside. She flings herself onto the leather couch and flips on the TV like she owns the place. I do a double take. There's a fireplace in the wall, the propane kind that goes on with a switch.

"Beds are back here," Dad says, pushing through a curtain.

Behind it, there's a small hallway with a regular-looking bathroom on one side and two narrow bunk beds built into the wall on the other. At the end, there's another door to a bedroom with a full-size bed, Dad's duffel thrown on top. I look at the bunks, each with its own window facing the swamp and a ruffled drape to close for privacy.

"Cozy," I say, not like I'm complaining, since an hour ago, I had pictured myself sleeping on the ground fending off critters all night.

"I knew you'd like it." Dad pats me on the back again. "Go ahead and wash up."

I can't wait to get out of this T-shirt and into my own clothes. Something more Survivor Girlish than "Sweet Treat Bake Shop." Maybe I'll wear the camouflage shirt with green and blue heart embellishments that Harper made for my birthday. She's a genius with rhinestones.

"Just don't change your shirt, Ali. You've already been on camera with it and if we were in the real wilderness, you wouldn't have a suitcase of fresh outfits."

"Seriously?" I say, because a new shirt is where my dad draws the line? Flat-screen TVs, full-size refrigerators, glossy floor and appliances, though — no problem. "But you don't mind if we sleep in this monstrosity on wheels?"

Dad's inspecting his teeth in the bathroom mirror. "Monstrosity on wheels isn't on camera."

I pull the General's book out of my bag and slide it under the pillow on the top bunk.

"But isn't it supposed to be all about surviving?" I

ask. "Like teaching people how to stay alive after a boat wreck in the middle of the Great Dismal Swamp or something? What would Grandpa say?"

He flicks the bathroom light off and strides past me to the front of the camper. "The General would be proud of what we've achieved. With more support on set, we can reach more people. Teach them how to survive in the most dangerous conditions, without endangering ourselves." He looks serious. "Maybe if he'd had a good crew, he'd never have disappeared."

"Who disappeared?" Isabel says, bouncing off the couch. "Is he dead?"

Dad puts a hand on my shoulder. "My father was the best survivalist I knew. I learned everything from him. But he took chances. Risks. And that's not something I'm willing to do. Not with two kids who are relying on me."

"And Mom, too," I say. "Don't forget about Mom."

"Sure." He stands up straight, swinging Isabel squealing onto his shoulders. "And your mom."

I think of the last time Mason Maguire accused my dad of being a fake, and how I told him the story of the sharks. I mean, Dad survived three days and two nights in shark-infested waters. He doesn't need all of this junk. He's just doing it this way for the family. For us. For me.

"Does the guy from *Me in the Wild* have all this stuff?" I ask.

"FACT!" Dad says. "That guy is a joke. Everyone knows he sleeps in a hotel."

A golf cart whizzes past the window, and when I look out I see half the crew sitting around picnic tables with cookies and coffee. I wonder for a minute if all of this luxury changes things. My dad is still my dad. Survivor Guy. So, does that make all of this okay?

Dad claps his hands. "Animal encounter time. Let's go."

We're back on the golf cart and I'm holding on for dear life with Isabel cutting the circulation off in my neck again. The animal encounter area is back by the medical tent, in the shade of the trees. Jake's still in bed, which is a good thing because the yellow flies are swarming. The crew has fashioned a kind of bug-trapper contraption out of a ball covered in black duct tape and sticky stuff hanging from a pole. It's working. The flies are all over it.

Dad parks next to a circle of trailers, probably

where the rest of the crew sleeps. They're not as nice as Dad's, but one of them has a door swung open and I spot a leather couch and flat-screen TV before Isabel grabs my hand and runs-hops-skips me toward the animals.

The trainer is decked out in a suit made of pillows, looking like a giant marshmallow, standing next to an overweight alligator in a large kiddie pool behind a fence.

"I want to feed him! I want to feed him!" Isabel yells.

I stop, stupefied once more. There are snakes in all sizes and shapes of evil stacked in plastic terrariums, a mountain lion, an alligator, a clear tub filled with fish, an aquarium full of mice, and two colorful birds in a cage. "Is this for real?" I say to Dad, as he strides right up to the mountain lion, who is casually squatting on a tree stump next to what looks like a dog house, in a giant chainlink enclosure. "I thought you said there weren't any alligators!"

"There aren't," Dad says. "That's why we had to bring one. It's my responsibility as Survivor Guy to show my audience what to do in case of an encounter with a deadly animal."

Marshmallow lady comes out of the enclosure, peeling her suit off, and hands me a hunk of raw meat. She nods to the alligator. "That's Lucy. She's super friendly."

"Throw it!" Isabel jumps up and down, clapping, and I lob it over the side of the pool, which hardly looks sturdy enough to hold back a newborn puppy. The alligator is sitting on a mound of sand surrounded by shallow water. It lunges and snaps at the treat.

"Samuel?" the animal trainer calls to Dad's stunt double, a clipboard in her hands. "I have you down for one snakebite on the edge of the lake this evening and a baby-bird rescue at sundown. Alison?"

I'm staring at the massive carnivorous beast of a mountain lion in front of me.

"Her name is Pudding," Isabel says. "Her favorite color is pink, like me."

"Alison?" The animal trainer waves me over, Isabel on my heels. "Rick? George? Is this right? I have Alison for an eight o'clock standoff with Lucy?"

"Excuse me?" I say. "As in, Lucy the alligator?"

Rick looks at his clipboard.

Dad now has a snake around his neck and is kissing it. What is wrong with him? If Grandpa saw him kissing a rattlesnake on the set of this so-called survivor show, he'd shake some sense into him right here and now. He might also fry up the rattler for supper. Supposedly they're high in fiber, and taste like tuna.

"Yes, that's correct." Dad puts a hand on my shoulder. "An alligator for my little Ali-Gator. Thank you, Laura."

"Uh, *what*?" I back away and trip over a root, falling hard onto the ground.

"Alison fell on her bum-bum!" Isabel squeals.

The camerawoman bolts over to me. "Show me agony! Defeat!" Rick calls.

I've got something I could show him, all right, but I count to ten and breathe through my nose like Dr. Tom says to do in Healthy Is Happy! It doesn't work.

I'm not surprised though, because basically nothing is working right anymore.

THIRTEEN

"*The big question,*" *Rick says,* "is can you climb a tree?" All of a sudden the rest of the crew is staring at me.

"Um, sure," I say, although I've never actually climbed one before. But I must have a ton of arm muscles from all the archery I've been doing. You can get muscles from archery, right?

"FACT! I've seen you scale that tree in the front yard a thousand times," Dad declares.

"Actually"—I swat a fly from my face—"that was Jake. Like ten years ago."

Adam must have walked up while I wasn't paying attention, because I hear him laugh behind me. And then everyone looks as if they're sizing me up, wondering if I'm as much of a Survivor Girl as I should be. Except for Isabel, of course, who keeps extending a hand to pet the mountain lion like it's a housecat, while Laura, the animal trainer, pushes her away.

"Let's go have a look then, shall we?" Rick says.

Everyone descends on the golf carts, four of them all lined up neatly next to the crew trailers. "Where are we going?" I say, trying to mask the desperation in my voice. Because am I going to have to climb a tree? Right now?

"It's all about safety here," the animal trainer says, sliding into the back seat with Adam. "If an alligator is going to chase you up a tree, we have to make sure you can climb that tree."

Isabel's crawling over me to get into the seat next to Dad again, all elbows and bony knees to my gut, talking on and on about the "big kitty" and how she looks sad in her cage.

"I don't think I have the right shoes," I say, pointing to my hiking boots. "I mean, look at them, they're clearly for tromping through lakes and—"

"They're perfect," the animal trainer says.

"Totally perfect," Adam chimes in, grinning.

And now my desperation turns to dread as the golf carts start up and zoom across the set and onto a tiny fire road behind the animal area. I don't even have a strategy. What's my strategy for tree climbing? There's nothing about tree climbing in Grandpa's book.

"I'll check the tree for critters first," the animal trainer says. "You know, snakes and poisonous spiders that like to hang out in the shade of the trees."

I'm sick. The little dinner that I had is burning a hole in my stomach. Did I just burp up orange fizz pizzazz?

"I have to go potty," Isabel shouts.

I regret all the mean thoughts I've ever had about her. "We should go back."

"Is it an emergency?" Dad asks.

"Of course it is!" I say. "You can't let her pee her pants!"

Isabel crosses her arms. "I don't pee in my pants. I can hold it."

The golf carts park next to a little red flag that says SURVIVOR GUY, stuck into the ground to the side of the fire road. Everyone else hops out, but I take a long time retying my shoes, until Rick calls me molasses and makes me get out of the vehicle.

We hike into the dense woods, my boots sinking

in the watery muck, until we come to a small clearing where there's a tall tree coming out of the bog.

"Let's roll camera," he says, motioning Bianca and Wes over, "but we're really just making sure the skill level here matches our expectations of the shot."

They're talking about *my* skill level. I look at Dad, feeling lightheaded, but he's playing swords with a tree branch.

Rick is studying the woods. "Let's use camera two as well."

Bianca whistles and a second camera guy trots over.

"So, say you were being chased by an alligator and you came into this small clearing. What would you do?" Rick says, talking to me again.

"Uh, run?" I look around, most of the crew staring at me. "Like, for my life?"

Rick steps closer. "Knowing that alligators can't climb trees, maybe you would . . ." He waits for me to answer.

"Climb a tree?"

Rick claps. "Yes! And, maybe you'd be coming from this direction, out of breath—or something—and then encounter this bog with the alligator nipping at your heels. You'd have to leap—make sure you're on the right foot—over the water and then climb this tree."

He gestures toward a swampy pool of water in the ground that, in all honesty, I probably couldn't even shoot an arrow over. Like, maybe if I were a giant gazelle with superpowers I could leap across it.

"Climb that tree with no branches?" I say.

"Just a suggestion." Rick massages his chin.

"Can I do it?" Isabel asks, raising her hand, jumping up and down.

"Whenever you're ready," Rick says, ignoring her, and everyone peels off to the sides of the clearing, leaving me a path to do my thing. All except for camera two, which is about an inch from my face. Bianca is at the other end by the mud pit, moving her camera from it to me. Do we really need to record this?

"Oh. Okay. No problem."

Dad gives me a thumbs-up and I inhale.

"One-two-three-GO!" Isabel says, and I just stand there because I'm not about to listen to some bossy little—

Rick pushes me in the shoulder. "Now is as good a time as ever! Just a suggestion."

I launch from my spot, picturing myself leaping a vast bog and climbing an unclimbable tree. Dr. Tom always says the key to success is visualization and determination, and maybe he's right, because the crew starts chanting my name, and I hear my dad say, "You can do this in your sleep, Survivor Girl!"

But what really gets me moving, past the paralyzing fear that when I try to leap over this bog I'll barely get off the ground before belly-flopping, is Adam's smirky face staring at me. He might think my dad's a fake, but not this girl. I'm no fake, and I'm just going to have to prove it to him.

I fly like an arrow and the running feels good. I feel fast, actually, my shoes slurping in the grass, spraying mud onto my legs. And I'm nearly at the bog, counting the steps until I need to jump. But then I remember that jumping is not my specialty. Not my specialty at all. And my feet are all wrong and my thighs are rubbing together and my shirt is hiking up.

I leap. It's pathetic. The opposite of a gazelle. My feet barely lift off the ground and I feel like I'm five hundred pounds. I manage to stop myself before hitting the water. "I tripped," I say, out of breath. "I think." Gasp. Sputter. "Tree root. Or something."

Rick is looking at my dad, who's looking at me, probably wondering where all his Survivor Guy genes went. For the millionth time today I wish it was just me and Dad and miles and miles of wilderness, because then maybe I could do it. There are just too many eyes and cameras and animal trainers watching.

"Can I pee in the woods?" Isabel asks, doing a serious potty dance, and everyone unfreezes from their thinking faces. The animal trainer takes her gloves off and whisks Isabel into the deep brush.

Rick claps. "Should we try again?"

But my body knows it's over and my brain wonders *what's the point?* I'll never be Survivor Girl. Fending off alligators. Eating crickets for lunch. Scaling trees like a professional. Just because I've read the General's words over and over to the point of memorizing doesn't mean I've got his skills.

They can see it in my face. I'm nothing like my dad and Grandpa and Jake. Nothing.

"On second thought," Rick says, checking his watch, "let's break. Maybe rethink the scenario."

We trudge back to the golf carts. "Wanna drive?" Dad says to me.

"I'd probably steer us off the road and into the swamp," I say.

Dad rubs my back. "Don't be so hard on yourself. Your legs are tired from the walk through the lake. We'll try again tomorrow."

Isabel comes busting out of the trees. "I peed in the woods!"

Everyone laughs and turns on their motors. "Congratulations, Isabel," Dad says.

And then she climbs into his lap and drives us home.

FOURTEEN

"Ali?" I hear Jake, back from the medical tent. "Ali?"

It's nighttime. After the bog episode, I told everyone I had a stomachache and had to lie down. There's
no phone service here. I've literally just been lying in
my bunk staring out the window at the crew running
back and forth with cameras and props and animals
in cages and snake bags. Isabel has knocked at least
thirteen times.

"Come on," Jake says. "Get up, you lazy butt!"

I should see if he's okay, but it's like I'm frozen on
my belly gazing out at the swamp. I have to crane my
neck to see the lake through the tiny bunk window,
and despite the name of this place, it's actually kind

of beautiful. I wonder if the alligator sees what I see from the tiny sand island in her pool. A Great Dismal Paradise. When the animal lady opens her door, why doesn't she just make a run for it?

"Ali," Jake says louder. I'm so good at ignoring him I can't stop, and I start to think he went away until his swollen red face peeks under my curtain. "We have a production meeting in the cottage."

"Should you even be out of bed?" I push him away.

"Maybe not, but I'm a fast healer." He flexes his muscles. "And Claire made me promise to take it easy for the rest of the night. So, come on. Get up."

I try to sit, bonking my head on the ceiling. Jake snickers.

"Maybe I don't want to go," I say, opening my curtain.

"All actors must be present." He reaches into a cabinet and pulls out a flappy piece of beef jerky. "That includes you."

I grimace and swing myself down from the bunk. "Ha. Actors." I huff.

Jakes chews with his mouth open. "What do you have against actors?"

My shirt is pulling up again and I stretch it so far down there's a ripping sound. "The whole point of the show is not to have actors."

"It's a TV show, Ali." Jake freezes with his hand in the jerky bag. "All TV shows have actors."

"A reality TV show. REALITY." I slip my sandals on. "But there's nothing real about it."

Jake snorts. "Reality TV is just as set up as regular TV. People aren't going to watch a show that doesn't tell a good story. Ask anyone."

It's like I'm the only one who didn't know. Betrayal, red-hot and burning, crawls up my body and pounds in my head. I think of all the times I've defended Dad. Once, in fourth grade, I even lost recess when I called Joshua a jerkface for saying Dad didn't really kill a bobcat with his bare hands and then revive it back to life. Episode 43, deep woods of Tennessee. He missed my Fourth of July Girl Scout parade for it. But who could get mad when he saved the life of a mama bobcat? I remember the mountain lion in the cage next to the alligator and it strikes me like a bolt of lightning. Had the bobcat been a lie too?

Jake stops chewing, staring at me. "This took him years to build. He started *Survivor Guy* as a web series. Just a tiny pocket camera and himself. Now look." He opens the door and the moist and earthy swamp air fills the camper. We watch the golf carts and the crew carrying boxes and binders, hurrying from one tent to the next with headlamps. "They're all getting ready for the big nighttime scene where Survivor Guy finds a sick bird by the lake."

"You mean his stunt double."

"This is TV, Alison. Show business." Jake shakes his head.

"Dad told me he was doing all this fake stuff for us, to keep safe so we'd still have him around. So that we wouldn't lose him like he lost Grandpa." I'm getting revved up now. "But what good is all that if he never comes home anymore? If he's so busy making TV shows for his fans that he's never around?"

"What do you think paid for the pool in our backyard? All your trips to the mall with what's-her-face?"

"Harper," I say.

"Dad's doing this for the money, Alison." Jake tosses the bag of jerky back in the cabinet. "The ratings. So you can have your fancy life."

"No he's not!" I yell, stopping Isabel as she skips past our camper. She peeks her head in and my face burns hotter. "He's doing this because Survivor Guy's in his blood. Just like Grandpa's."

"It's like you're in your own world. You only believe what you want to believe. Just like Mom and Dad breaking up—"

I brush past him, bumping him with my shoulder, and storm out of the camper. Isabel backs away.

"It's not nice to yell," she calls.

Jake's right beside me and he does a showoffy leap across the little creek that cuts our camp in half while I thump across the bridge.

"You're just like him, Ali. I've heard you talk to your friends about how you go on adventures with Dad. How you're an awesome Survivor Girl." We race past the dining tent. "How is that reality?"

I ignore him, walking even faster, around the portable bathhouses—which are air conditioned and called honey wagons, by the way—to the little cottage with the giant screened-in porch. It's the only permanent structure here, an old house left over from when this place was a wilderness campground.

"Dad's not the only one good at living a lie," Jake says, holding the door open for me.

"You're just being mean," I say, and then I stomp hard on his foot as I pass, making him yelp. I'm so angry, I can barely breathe. How can he say *I'm* living a lie?

Inside there are wood floors, and couches and chairs in front of a giant stone fireplace. Tables are covered with computer screens and expensive-looking electronics. Samuel is sitting in a comfortable-looking armchair and Dad is sprawled out on a love seat sipping a steaming mug of frothy coffee. "Want a hot chocolate, Ali?" he says, but then seeing my face — "Not feeling better?"

Jake sighs. "I told you not to bring her on set! She wants you to be like Grandpa and get yourself lost in the Alps."

I punch him hard in his muskie bite. "I didn't say that."

Adam and Rick walk in, heavy with bags, their arms loaded with folders and papers. I stop talking.

"Ali-Gator. We're still the real deal over here. We're just taking precautions and making sure everyone is comfortable and safe." Dad wipes froth from his lips.

"Maybe you should change your slogan then," I say, trying not to look at Adam, who I'm sure has some annoying smirk on his face.

Dad laughs. "Remember when we tried that, Rick?"

"When we tried what?" Rick asks, passing us each a clipboard.

"You know." Dad slurps his coffee. "The one guy, one camera thing."

"Great slogan," Rick says. "But do you know how hard it is to walk in dangerous terrain while trying to videotape too?"

I can feel Adam staring at me. I use my clipboard like a fan, my face still on fire from Jake's rude accusations. Sure, I've let a few friends think I'm really great at surviving in the wild. So what? That's nowhere near as bad as having my own reality show that's as far from reality as possible.

Dad bursts out laughing, nearly spilling his drink as he pulls himself up and off the couch. "Remember in the Oklahoma grasslands when I fell into the ravine trying to walk backwards and tape the sunset?" Rick is hysterical now too, the giggles moving to Jake and Samuel and even a little bit to Adam. Not me though. I'm wondering what I was doing while Dad was tromping through some prairie pretending to be someone he's not. Did I have a dance recital? An archery tournament? Maybe it was even my birthday?

Adam hands out packets of papers. Mine has my name on the top. "Notes." It's as thick as Grandpa's guidebook.

"Just some ideas to get us thinking about tomorrow's shoot." Rick sits next to Dad on the couch, wiping his eyes. "Ali, we're thinking our audience will see you as the unlikely heroine. Scared, unskilled, weak—"

"Hey!" I interrupt.

Adam snorts.

"It's part of the story line, Ali-Gator, for the story," Dad says. "How you'll be portrayed on camera."

I roll my eyes teenage-angst style. "I should be myself on reality TV."

Rick and Dad and Jake are all looking at each other like I'm an idiot child. "This is reality TV, Alison," Dad says. "Reality TV is not always about the real reality, but the perception of reality."

He slurps his coffee again.

"Let's take a look at the notes," Rick repeats, standing up and clapping his hands. "George, start us off. Page one."

Dad puts his coffee down and his face changes to serious Survivor Guy. "Night one. Little sleep with the threat of bears and wolves and swarms of yellow flies."

"Jake wakes up," Jakes announces from where he's laid out on an overstuffed chair.

Rick has been intently watching Dad read, like he's watching an artist at work. "Don't read the action notes, Jake. Continue, George."

"The flies have gotten the best of my boy, Jake, but I've collected some midnight mud from the bottom of the lake and concocted this lifesaving salve. No big deal, just the result of years and years of learning to survive in this wild world we live in. It will relieve his swelling and reverse the allergic reaction."

Next, it says ALISON AWAKENS, WIDE-EYED, JUMPY FROM THE SOUNDS OF THE SWAMP, HER HAIR BRAIDED. "DADDY! DADDY! I'M SO SCARED! PLEASE SAVE ME FROM THIS DANGEROUS SWAMP!"

"Is this my line?" I ask. "Do I have to say this?"

Rick shakes his head. "No. Alison, my dear, this

is an unscripted show." He waves the papers in the air. "Notes. Just suggestions."

They're all looking at me, Dad frozen in a Survivor Guy stare. Do I look that scared and weak and uncoordinated? The actual reality of the situation is that probably my friends won't be surprised at all when they find out I'm not a Survivor Girl hero. I can barely make it through skill testing in gym. In fact, Harper and I tie for last every single time. Out of the entire grade.

So, I read the suggested line. But I don't embrace this scared and weak character. In fact, I pretty much hate her right now.

FIFTEEN

The next morning when I stumble out of the camper, Isabel is standing there with a pink sprinkled doughnut, wearing a purple nightgown with prancing white horses all over it. "For you!"

"Have you been waiting here all morning?" I say, taking the doughnut, because if I didn't it would be rude, right?

"You sleep a lot."

Laura, the animal trainer, walks by with a snake around her neck, carrying a plastic bag full of little fish. The camp is bustling with activity as if it's not just barely past sunrise. There's a guy cutting wood by the crew trailers, people pushing carts stacked high with equipment, and a line going into the dining tent.

Dad is at the bank of the lake surrounded by Producer Rick, Medic Claire, Immature Intern Adam, and Camera Lady Bianca. He is struggling, trying to make a homemade fishing hook out of a sharp rock he found. Eventually a prop guy hands him a professionally homemade fishing rod with a rock-ish-looking hook. I turn away. I can't take any more of the fakeness.

"Why is your mom there?" I say to Isabel. I mean, I'd probably need a medic on duty if I was trying to fish with a razor-sharp hook made out of jagged rock, but not Dad. I'm pretty sure he at least knows how to fish.

"She's always with him." Isabel licks pink frosting off her pinky finger. "They're best friends forever."

I take a monstrous bite out of my doughnut.

"Just like I'm going to have a trillion best friends when I go to kindergarten. They don't even have cameras there, did you know that?"

I take another bite, my mouth so full I can barely breathe except through my nose.

"A trillion, trillion, ka-million maybe. And my friends will teach me how to play games and sometimes we'll fight over the last Lego." She twirls around. "That's what kids do, right? Play Legos?"

I'm still chewing.

"And I don't even know what I'm going to be for Halloween yet."

I wipe my mouth on my arm, watching Isabel's mom untangle part of the fishing line and hand it to my dad. "Well," I say. "Sometimes it's not nice to have best friends because then everyone else feels left out." Claire reaches up and smooths my dad's hair and I almost choke. "Actually, sometimes it's super mean and disgusting."

Isabel just looks at me, shielding her eyes from the sun. And then she grabs my hand. "C'mon." She pulls me to the edge of the lake as I stuff the last of the doughnut in my mouth.

Adam is busy hooking a flailing swamp muskie to the fake homemade fishing line when Isabel and I walk up. "Ali-Gator!" Dad says, and squeezes us into a hug. Isabel smells like candy ChapStick and little-kid nail polish, and when I finally get out of the huddle of death, there's frosting on my elbow.

Adam hands Dad his homemade fishing rod he didn't make with the fish on it that he didn't catch. The muskie is snapping and flopping.

"Breakfast!" Dad points to the fish, and then looks past us to the dining tent. "No, actually, what's for breakfast today?"

"Doughnuts!" Isabel shrieks.

I notice Adam and Rick talking and looking in my direction. I stand straighter, smoothing my shirt down and pushing my wild hair out of my face. I've just discovered a spot of crusty pink frosting on my cheek when they come walking up to me.

"The alligator scene," Rick says. "We need to get that nailed down ASAP." He folds his arms, a finger to his lips. "Or—hey, George! What if we took that scene in a different direction? Like, Alison falls into the bog or something. Would that feel more natural to you, Alison?" Rick is pacing, back and forth, tapping his head.

Dad joins him. "And I save her?"

"Yes!" Rick snaps his fingers. "Yes! Hero dad

comes along and wrestles the alligator into submission and rescues his daughter from the mud pit. That would be amazing!" Dad and Rick congratulate each other on their new genius idea.

"No," I interrupt. "No way. *I* want to be the hero." I may not be the world's best tree climber, but in real life I'm not the kind of girl that needs to be rescued all the time.

Dad smiles big, nodding his head. "My girl, the hero. I like it."

Rick is tapping his head again. "So, no mud-pit alligator rescue?" He sighs.

"You're making me out to be all weak and scared all the time. It's not fair," I add.

Adam is smirking. At least, I think he's smirking. He just always looks like a jerk.

"Okay." Rick's eyes are closed. "No mud-pit rescue, girl saves herself from man-eating alligator . . ." He's mumbling to himself. ". . . leaps over . . . tree . . ." He opens his eyes. "That still plays well into the unlikely hero story. Also, girl power. Our audience will love it. Brilliant! Great idea, Ali."

I ignore the unlikely hero part. "Thanks," I say, and Dad kisses my forehead.

"Okay, son, take Ali to the scene location and see if you can give her some tree-climbing tips, okay?" Rick claps Adam on the back.

We watch Rick walk away and then Adam kind of saunters off, like this is the worst assignment in the history of assignments.

"Why does he always call you son?" I ask, following him to the back of the set, where the animals are already awake in their cages, all except for the mountain lion, who has a single sleepy paw sticking out of her dog house.

"None of your business," Adam says, jumping into a golf cart and rolling it out of the parking spot.

"Hey! Wait!" It's not like I want to go anywhere with him, but what choice do I really have?

Adam halts the cart and looks at me. "Bus is leaving." And then he takes off again, but there is no way I'm chasing after him, because this girl doesn't chase after boys. Except maybe Justin Barbara that time he stole my limited-edition pumpkin pie ChapStick right out of my hands.

Adam stops the cart and my brain knows as soon as I start walking in his direction he'll take off. But apparently my legs don't get the message because they start walking, and just when I'm about to grab on and heft myself into the seat, he punches the accelerator.

"That's it!" I start walking back to the lake. "I'm telling Dad and then he'll fire you as intern."

He does a U-turn, rolling the golf cart alongside of me. "Fine. You're no fun. Get in."

"I'm still telling him." I keep walking, my arms crossed. "Why are you such a jerk, anyway? Probably every kid in America would pay a bajillion dollars to be Survivor Guy's intern."

He grunts, rolling his eyes. "It's not like you're the nicest person in the world. Why are you so mean to Isabel? This is her life. Moving from wilderness set to wilderness set. All the time." He waves toward all the tents and trailers and *Survivor Guy* equipment everywhere. There must have been a bit of rain overnight, because everything is a little muddy, including my hiking boots. And the heat mixing with the smell of doughnuts and swamp isn't the greatest. "She doesn't even know what a Barbie is. I asked her."

"Barbies are overrated." I flick a gnat off my arm.

"Come on. Just get in," Adam says.

I don't even look at him.

"I'm going to tell your dad that you volunteered

for the live-snake-eating scene. Live. Snake. In your belly." He licks his lips.

"He won't believe you," I say, but the truth is Dad barely even knows me lately. And maybe he'd do anything for ratings. For the money. Forget about me, his own daughter.

"They're getting desperate for volunteers." He tries pulling in front of me, but I swerve around him. "They want to introduce your character with a bang, don't forget. Wabam! Snake-eating girl. That's network-worthy if you ask me."

I stop. "Let's just get this over with." I climb into the golf cart, but I sit in the back, teetering on one of the jump seats that's half taken up by a giant card-board box.

"Careful, there are snapping turtles in there."

But when I peek inside, I see they're just made of plastic.

SIXTEEN

When we park on the fire road, I don't even let the golf cart stop before I jump out and barrel into the woods, leaving Adam trying to catch up. I've collected all of my frustrations in my body and pushed them deep into my muscles. Dad and his new BFF. Little annoying kids. Camerawomen and interns. Lies. Lies. Lies. Who even has a BFF when you're like fifty years old?

I get to the clearing and the tree is dead ahead, branchless, centered in front of a bog and impossible to climb. I take off running, because with so much angst I'm going to soar over that mud pit like it doesn't even exist. Soar, I tell you. I'm two strides away and my legs are strong and ready. I leap. I soar.

Then I cannonball into the middle of the bog, dousing myself in brown swamp water. My muscles spasm and I limp out, ignoring Adam's tittering.

He stands at the edge of the mud pit and jumps it easy as pie. No running starts. No angsty muscles. He is the king of gazelles.

"Ladies first," he says, pointing to the tree.

"Oh, I insist." I extend my muddy arm like a fancy model on a game show. "You first."

He springs into action, wrapping his legs and arms around the tree and shimmying halfway up, then dropping back down in front of me. "Easy."

I cross my arms and spin away from him.

"What are you so angry about anyway? Just admit you can't do it and we can move on."

I push him out of the way and march to the tree. "Aren't you supposed to be teaching me?"

"Just wrap yourself around the trunk and boost yourself up. Simple."

I stare at the tree. And I hate it. I hate the rushy-throbby-heartbeat feeling like I'm in gym class trying to climb the rock wall. It takes me half the period to get to the top while everyone else flies up, effortless.

Adam sighs. "Let me see your muscles." He pokes me in the arm, where—let's be honest—I don't have any muscles.

"Ow!"

"Yeah, no, you can't do it." He squeezes my weak bicep, mystified, like it's some wonder of the world.

"Hey!" I put my hands on my hips, getting in his face. "I can do anything."

"Not really." Adam shrugs his shoulders like he's not insulting me to my face. "If you don't do the work, you can't do just anything." He flexes his bicep. "Wabam! I lift weights every day. Even on Christmas."

"There's more to life than working out, you know." I put one foot on the side of the tree, digging in with my hiking boot, ready to boost myself up.

"Parents always tell their kids they can do anything. But actually it's not true. You can't just wake up one day and . . ." I tune out his braggy voice and try to hoist myself up enough to get my other foot on the tree.

". . . people don't climb Mount Everest or win the Nobel Peace Prize without a ton of . . ."

And I'm up. A little bit. Shaky and muscles burning, but I'm at least an inch off the ground.

". . . your dad could totally do the real Survivor Guy thing in the real wild and stuff. Except it's too hard. Too much work. So, he takes a shortcut . . ."

I glare at him and he throws his hands up. "No offense. I mean, it's totally what everyone does."

I stumble off the tree, just barely missing the mud pit again, my entire body pulsing. "He could be the real type of Survivor Guy if he wanted."

"I literally just said that. Were you even listening?"

"Well, in case you're interested, my dad has such a big crew and stuff for safety." I shake my head at him. "So he can always be there for me."

"Dads say those things all the time and they're always full of —"

"Not my dad. Nope. He's all about family." My belly burns because with only half the family home all the time, it's like a puzzle missing pieces. And once you lose a piece to a puzzle, it's worthless. It's barely even a puzzle anymore.

"Your dad is just like my dad. He doesn't care about family." Adam breaks a stick in half. "He just cares about ratings. That's why they're such a good team."

"Team?" I say, and then it dawns on me. "Rick? The producer? That's your dad?"

There's a rustling in the thick brush bordering the clearing we're in and Adam and I freeze and stare at each other.

Snake? Swamp rodent?

Leaves crunching. Branches snapping.

Bear? Panther?

I swing around, looking for a place to hide, wishing I had a can of Survive-A-Bear. Adam grabs for me, but I hightail it for a tree in the denser part of the woods, the rustling getting closer and louder. There are a lot of branches on this one and I climb. The first branch cracks off under my weight but I manage to pull myself onto a thicker, higher branch, where I stay, one leg dangling. Awkwardly.

Two kids pop out of the woods. One of them screams when she sees me, the other one blinks behind his bug helmet. I nearly lose my balance and fall.

"Snakes live in these trees, you know," the girl

says, shading her eyes and coming over to stand at the base of mine. "Are you with Kids on Adventure?"

"What?" My muscles are seizing up. "No." I look for Adam and find him shimmying down from the branchless tree by the bog like he's a superhero or something.

"You're just here by yourself?" the boy asks, but then he sees Adam and bounces into a ninja stance.

"Relax, he's with me." I nod toward Adam. "I wouldn't say he's the nicest guy in the world, but . . ."

"Adam." He thrusts a hand in the bug helmet boy's direction and they shake.

"Theo. And this is Ronnie." Ronnie takes a bow.

They're not seeing me at my best angle, my butt hanging out over the tree branch. I try to leap down but my foot is actually stuck. Fabulous.

"You should get down," Theo says.

"Just doing some research," I reply.

My other leg is tingling now and I try to let it slide a bit down the trunk, except I've lost all muscle control and can't stop it from skidding all the way to the ground. So now I'm standing on one foot with the other wedged into the crook of the branch and I'm in excruciating pain since I'm not the most flexible person in the world.

"Are you okay?" Ronnie pulls my stuck foot out of my shoe and I flop back into the moist dirt, but I'm up before either of them come at me with concerned faces again. They mostly just look confused—except for Jerk Adam . . . who looks delighted.

"Wait." Theo takes a step back. "Are you?" He glances at his friend like he's asking her something telepathically. Harper and I can do that. I telepathically communicate to her my ice cream order while I hold our seats at Dilly's every time.

"Survivor Guy's daughter from the Pop-Tarts picture!" they say in unison.

They're talking about that picture of Dad and me in the celebrity magazine. Eating Pop-Tarts by the lake. "That was like a year ago." I wipe my muddy hands on my shorts, because there's no point in trying to look clean anymore.

They're jumping up and down and Ronnie is clapping. "I can't believe this!" she says. "We love that show!"

"Wait, are you guys taping here?" Theo looks around like he half expects Dad to jump out of a tree.

In reality, he's probably moved on to breakfast by now, eating a jelly doughnut and sipping a cappuccino.

"Shut up!" Ronnie yells. "Our counselors said someone's filming in the swamp, but they didn't say it was *Survivor Guy*! Like, the actual *Survivor Guy*?" She looks like she's about to faint, or at least dunk herself by accident into the puddle she's teetering over.

"He's back at camp." I motion in the general direction of the set.

"Can we come see?" Ronnie asks, handing me my shoe, which she's managed to pull out of the tree.

My leg cramps from all the running and climbing and leaping over mud pits and I struggle to stand upright and look normal while my muscles bunch into a knot. I find a stump and hop over to it, trying to massage my leg. I put my shoe back on, my sock already soaked through with mud, and is that a tadpole stuck to it? "I wish I could take you to the set, but—"

"Too dangerous?" Theo says.

"Yes," I nod my head. "Absolutely what I was going to say."

Adam snorts.

Ronnie starts to examine the clearing, pulling

up rocks and rolling logs over. "We're at archaeology camp," she says. "Looking for evidence of old communities."

I don't pretend to know what she's talking about.

"This swamp used to hide whole groups of men, women, and children who escaped slavery and some other people too probably," Theo says.

Ronnie grabs a twig from the ground, shaking off the dirt. "It was a stop on the Underground Railroad, you know."

Betsy Sue had said that, too. I eye the trees, wondering how many ghosts haunt these woods.

Theo holds out a squirmy millipede he found under a leaf. "Do you have to eat stuff like this?"

I look at Adam, who is staring at me.

"We've been living on camp food for two weeks," Theo says, jiggling the millipede. "Half-cooked oatmeal, stale granola, peanut butter."

"What do they feed you on *Survivor Guy*? Berries and grass or something?" Ronnie is practically clapping. "What's your favorite edible insect?"

I think about what Jake said. How I lie to my friends. But the honest truth is, I don't lie that much, and it's always for a good cause, like to avoid dashing the dreams of a *Survivor Guy* fan or something.

"Grasshopper, probably," I say. The gummy kind from the nature center gift shop. I stand up and stretch. "Mice too." It's not a complete lie. Because I read in the notes that someone on set will have to eat a mouse cooked over an open flame at some point. It just won't be me.

"Personally, I had a doughnut this morning for breakfast." Adam pats his belly. "Chocolate with rainbow sprinkles, and I even asked the chef for a little squirt of whipped cream."

Ronnie and Theo stare at him. I break the silence by launching into a fit of laughter that comes out more like cackling. But it works, because soon Ronnie, Theo, and I are all laughing together at Adam's joke that's not really a joke.

"You poor things. You'd probably die for a peanut butter sandwich right now." Ronnie pulls something out of the dirt and holds it up to Theo. "Arrowhead?"

"Rock," he says, batting it out of her hand.

I hear the producer's whistle in the distance calling everyone to set for a scene.

"What was that?" Theo says. "Did you hear that?"

"Is that your dad sending out an alert?" Ronnie asks.

"Well, we should probably get back," I say. "It was great meeting you guys." I pull at my shirt and start walking backwards.

They wave. "Will we see you again?" Ronnie asks.

"Sure, okay, maybe," I reply.

We watch Ronnie and Theo leave the same way they came, and then Adam turns to me. "You're just like your dad."

He's the second person to say that to me since I've gotten here. A few days ago, I would have thought it was a compliment, but somehow now it feels like a burn.

He storms off into the woods toward the golf cart and we drive back in silence.

SEVENTEEN

Isabel is first to greet us back at camp, sitting cross-legged in the middle of the fire road. She has a stick in her hand and she's surrounded herself with pebbles.

"Hey!" she calls, getting up and running alongside of the golf cart. "Did he teach you how to climb a tree? Adam, can you teach me to climb a tree? Do they teach that in kindergarten? One time Adam gave me a piece of gum. Look! I can almost tie my shoe!" She drops to the ground, pulling at her shoelaces while we drive past her and park.

Adam turns off the ignition and stalks away. Dad and Jake are huddled over a pile of wood by the shore of the lake with Rick. Isabel catches up to me, breathing heavy. "I have to show you something."

Since I don't feel like staring at a pile of wood with Jake and Dad, I follow her, feeling my biceps for muscles. I wonder how many days of working out it would take for me to get as fit as Adam. Five? Ten? A thousand? I pick up a big rock and do some lifting action like I'm in a gym, but then my arm starts burning and I need some water and maybe even a snack, so I throw it back to the ground.

"Pudding!" Isabel points to the black mountain lion, sleeping in the sun like a housecat in her enclosure. Her tail flicks as we walk past like maybe she's not all the way asleep.

Isabel opens a cooler and pulls out a chunk of fish. She holds her nose with one hand and tosses the fish at Pudding with the other. The mountain lion rouses, strides over to the treat, and gobbles it up, her pink sequin collar glinting in the sun.

"Fish is her favorite." Isabel leans on the chainlink fence that barely separates us from the man-eating predator. "I told her for Christmas I'll get her a whole pond of fish or maybe even an ocean. She's four just like me, but we don't have the same birthday."

"Ali-Gator!" Dad calls to me from the lake, waving his arm.

Isabel whirls around and takes off toward my dad like he's calling her name instead. But I'm right behind her, running hard because even though Isabel has stumpy four-year-old legs, they're fast. I pass her, sticking out my tongue, and she giggles, thinking this is all a game. I run faster.

When I get to the lake, trying not to gasp for air, I realize Bianca has been taping my sprint across the set. And now she's in my face, Wes clicking on his digital sound recorder and positioning the boom over my head. "Reactions to seeing the live bear drinking water from the lake with her new cub. Go."

"Bear?" I wheeze. "What bear?"

Isabel bounds into the group, nearly toppling over what looks like the start of a campfire, and launches into her mom's arms. Bianca swings the camera away from me, focusing on Dad, who starts in with his Survivor Guy voice. "Having two kids in the swamp is risky. Dangerous. Even life-threatening." He freezes, looking over his shoulder like something's there. Isabel's the opposite of frozen, dancing near the water's edge, going full-body slump when Claire tries to pick her up and drag her away. "FACT!!" Dad says. "The Great Dismal Swamp is home to many wild animals.

Bears. Panthers. Alligators. Hungry, desperate animals." Dad puts his arm on my shoulder. "Breathe, sweetheart, breathe. I won't let them get you." Dad whips out a can of his bear spray, the words HUMANS RULE, BEARS DROOL big and bold above his *Survivor Guy* insignia. He holds it out, ready to shoot.

"Perfect." Rick raises his hand. "Just perfect. Great father-daughter bonding."

Adam stares at me as he hands Dad a bottle of water. "You're a natural at acting, Alison. Like in every situation," Adam says.

"Yessir!" Rick agrees, clapping me on the back. "Sure is."

I sneer at Adam because I know what he means and I am far from appreciating it. When I turn around, Jake pops out in front of me. "Boo!"

"Ahhhh!" I scream. His face is smeared with dirt and hives and—is that blood? And I'm not proud of it because a second later I realize it's makeup.

"That's literally the best compliment anyone could give me," a lady says, shaking my hand. "I'm the makeup supervisor. Can I cover those up for you?" She inspects the cluster of stress zits on my chin.

And I submit to the makeup-ing, sitting on a big

rock, the lake nearly lapping my feet. The sun is too strong for the yellow flies to come out just yet, but the breeze is cool on my sweaty skin. I watch Rick and Adam talking by the trees. Rick tries to put an arm across Adam's shoulder, but he ducks away. It makes me think of Mom and how I didn't even say I love you when she left. Rick's walking back to the trailers now, alone, and the look on his face leaves my stomach panging. Why didn't I just say I love you?

The makeup lady holds a mirror in front of my face and I gasp. I look dreadful, but in a bedraggled-naturally-gorgeous way. Like I've just been found on a deserted island that had a professional makeup artist.

"Wow," I say, touching a scratch made entirely of makeup on my neck. "I love it." My eyes are dark and brooding. It's like I'm this mysterious Survivor Girl who can make a fishnet out of woven grass and leaves and save everyone from starvation. I look like that kind of girl. I can't wait to take a picture and show it to Harper.

"You got a boyfriend back home?" makeup lady asks, applying a third layer of mascara to my already heavy eyelashes.

I look over by the trees and see that Adam's watching, chomping his gum. "Yeah," I say, and I know it's not entirely true since Brad Garrison hasn't officially asked me to be his girlfriend, but if Harper and I had gone to the sixth-grade dance and Brad hadn't taken Lilly van Stumen, then he'd probably have asked me to dance for sure. And if that's not an almost-pretty-much boyfriend, I don't know what is.

"You're gonna knock him dead," she says.

EIGHTEEN

It's early afternoon and Jake, Dad, and I are sitting at the edge of the lake. I ignore the crew standing silent a few feet behind us because this feels real. The three of us just hanging out.

But then Dad whispers loudly, "We'll need to seek shelter tonight. You know we can't stay here, right, Ali?" And the moment is over; we're back in *Survivor Guy* mode. Jake flops back onto the sand, resting his head against Dad's leg. Dad scoops up some of his homemade salve made from caterpillar guts and lake scum and dabs Jake's hives with it. Jake winces ever so slightly.

"Alison." It's Rick, over my shoulder. "Maybe you

feel worried for your brother, right? He's in a bad state, his body still fighting a bad reaction. The danger is real. Maybe you worry if he's going to make it at all."

I play along. "Dad?" I ask. "Is Jake going to make it?" I look at him, and he does look terrible, his skin still red and swollen a bit. What if the yellow flies came right now? Jake's not even covered up.

"FACT!!" Dad says. "All we need is this knife"— he pulls out a rusted-up *Survivor Guy*-brand knife from his waistband—"and that bear spray—"

I struggle to find the bear spray Dad points at, but then I see the fluorescent pink can among the twigs and moss we've collected for our nighttime shelter. "You mean this one, Dad?" I hold it up.

Dad stands, carefully removing Jake's head from his lap, holds his arms out wide, and closes his eyes. "I don't want to scare you, Ali, but the yellow flies are near. I can feel it."

I look at the approaching clouds and, for real, I can picture the yellow flies swarming us, merciless.

"Then should we get out of here?" I say, halfway meaning it. "Jake's not even wearing any protective bug gear."

"FACT! Yellow flies are not active at night." Dad licks the tip of his finger and holds it up in the wind that's not really there. "We will build a shelter inland and wait until nightfall."

Dad tries to rouse Jake, but he's pretending to be out cold.

"Ouch!" Dad smacks his arm. "Too late. They're here." He cups a dead yellow fly in his hands that the prop guy tossed to him off camera. It's small and yellow, like a bee but without the stripes.

"Ali." Rick's back and whispering to me again. "So, like, if you knew there were a bunch of yellow flies coming and there was nowhere to run, think about what you'd do. How would you protect your *only* brother?"

"Uh." I look around. Half the crew is behind us, watching, while the rest of camp is going on with their regular business. Isabel is doing cartwheels by the medical tent and the chef is pushing a cart of melons into the dining area. I turn back to the lake. "Oh, maybe pull him into the water?"

Rick gestures for me to go ahead, so I yank Jake's ankle with all of my strength.

"Use your soccer muscles, Ali! I'm under attack!"

Dad whirls around, fighting off the horde of yellow flies. "Get yourselves to safety!"

I know he means archery muscles, but I don't correct him. I pull Jake, who is dead weight. I jab him in his ribs. "Come on. Help me." He doesn't, so I push him to a sitting position and grab his limp arm, throw it over my shoulder, and heft him upright.

"Faster, Ali!" Dad shrieks. "They're swarming! Go!"

Jake's not even supporting his weight anymore and he falls back to the beach where Dad is flailing. I scoop water and douse Jake, who jumps a little and opens his eyes for a second to give me a look.

"It's not working! He needs to be in the lake!" Dad screams.

My throat is burning, because what if this was actually happening? What if we didn't have fancy camping trailers or bug hats right behind the cameras? What would I do? Could I save Jake if I really needed to?

I pull harder and harder, inching him closer to the lake and the safety of the water. And then with one final tug, and a little help from Jake, we are both in the cool dark water of Lake Drummond.

The crew claps.

Jake leaps out toward Adam, who is holding two towels, leaving me panting in the brown water. Adam delivers my towel and I manage to wrap myself up. Dad strides over and gives me a big hug. "You were great, Ali-Gator. Really great."

"Great stuff," Rick agrees. "Let's reconvene at the site of the shelter build in five. Ali, you can sit this one out since we have you scavenging for edible plants off camera while Jake and your dad build the shelter." I pull the towel from my head and Rick ruffles my wet hair. "Take a break. You deserve it."

I wander into the dining tent, my stomach grumbling. It's a little after two o'clock, just about the time Harper and I would be settling in for Healthy Is Happy! with Dr. Tom at school. And then we'd make gagging and choking and fighting-off-death signals to each other when he passed out the kale chips or fig bars or whatever snack he tortured us with that day. Missing Harper feels like a stitch in my gut.

"Teatime in thirty minutes!" the chef says when he sees me.

"Oh." I inhale, taking in an aroma of warm sweetness. "Sure, okay."

"Homemade pop tarts." He signals to the rickety kitchen setup in the back of the tent.

I freeze in place. "Pop tarts? Homemade?"

The chef laughs. "Your dad said they're your favorite," he says, walking toward the ovens.

"He's got that right." Leave it to my dad to get my pastry preferences correct but not even know the sport I'm currently kicking butt in.

He brings back a plate with a single pop tart, steamy and oven-crisped, placing it on the table in front of me. "You can be my taste-tester."

I plop into a chair and blow gently across the pastry. The chef squeezes a dollop of icing onto it, which streams over the edges, glazing the top perfectly. "Are you some kind of chef genius?" I say, because —homemade pop tarts.

He laughs and pulls up a chair next to me. "I love it when crew kids are around. You guys make everything so fun."

"Does Isabel always come on shoots?" I ask, taking a drippy bite of deliciousness. Cinnamon sugar. My favorite.

"She's practically grown up on set. She adores your father."

I take a giant bite, the filling burning my tongue.

"Adam's kind of new around here. He's got some quirks and doesn't fully appreciate my cooking, but he's growing on me." He smiles.

"His dad's the producer, huh?" I say with a full mouth.

"Complicated thing those two have," the chef says. "But I guess that's what happens when you don't see each other for four years."

"Four years?"

Isabel bursts into the tent. "Pop tarts! My favorite!" Shouldn't she be taking a nap or something?

"Not yet, little one," the chef says. "Few more minutes." But then his timer goes off and he's up and out of his chair, hustling over to his ovens.

"Ali," he calls. "Help me frost these and then take a tray over to the production tent?" He pulls cookie sheets out of the oven. "They're supposed to be enjoyed toasty warm."

"Don't have to tell me that!" I say, licking my fingers, but really wondering in my mind about Adam. Four years?

Isabel flies at me and wraps her body around one of my legs. "Koala bear! Koala bear!" she shrieks.

I pretend to ignore her and drag her along with me to the kitchen area, as she giggles and laughs and only holds tighter.

"Good with kids, too?" the chef says, poking Isabel in the nose and leaving a dollop of icing behind. "Your dad always says you're good at everything."

I'm busy trying to wedge Isabel off my leg, which is slowly losing feeling, but I stop. "He said that?"

"He misses you a lot when he's on set. Must be absolutely in heaven with you here with him."

I help the chef squeeze icing onto the homemade pop tarts and then carry a giant plastic tray of them across the Dismal Swamp, over the little bridge, and into the cottage where Dad and Jake and the rest of the crew are huddled around the TV monitors. Isabel grabs the tray from my hands, nearly dumping everything to the dirt floor, so she can hand them out herself. They dive at the treats.

But not even Isabel can get me upset, because what I see playing on the screen is me pulling Jake into the lake. And even though Jake helped move himself down the beach a bit, the way the camera was angled, it looks just like I was the hero little sister. Like I rescued Jake from the grip of death.

"Looking good," Dad says, snagging a second pop tart. "Very proud of you, Alison. I always knew you'd be a natural at this."

I continue to watch myself as they edit the footage. My mud-streaked bakery shirt actually looks cool. And don't even get me started on my eye makeup.

I picture Harper and the rest of my friends watching my *Survivor Guy* episode and a tiny maybe-bubble swells in my belly. Maybe I've been worrying for nothing. Maybe I'll look like a natural out here. Kicking butt in the Great Dismal Swamp. And maybe I'll be a hero when I get home just like Dad and Jake, and everyone will ask me what it's like to be a Survivor Girl. And they'll want interviews and they'll ask me how I got to be so good at being awesome in the unforgiving wilderness. Maybe it's okay to let people believe what they want to believe every once in a while.

What's so wrong with that?

NINETEEN

Nobody else is up yet when I roll out of my bunk and put on my mud-soaked Survivor Girl clothes and slide my compass into my pocket, super-stealth silent so Jake and Dad don't wake up. I tiptoe out of the camper and straight to the parked golf carts, grabbing the first one I see. I take a breath, reminding myself that if Adam is capable of driving a golf cart, then I definitely am too. When I turn the key in the ignition, the engine sounds loud in the early morning, and at first I can't even figure out how to get it out of park. But then I find the right lever and I'm off, driving down the fire road like a pro.

I brake at the little red SURVIVOR GUY flag marking the spot and march through the bushes, not even stopping for thorns or possible spiderwebs. My tree and bog are still there, barely visible through the mass of swamp brush. It's my last chance to defeat them. If Survivor Girl can drag a two-hundred-pound brother into Lake Drummond with barely any help at all, she can leap a mud pit and climb a branchless tree.

The bog is within reach now and the maybe-bubble in my stomach is solid. Maybe this is it. Maybe this time, I conquer. I don't even warn my body, just launch into a running start and sail—Survivor Girl style—over the pit of mud. I splash down on the other side, landing on my feet. Steady. First try.

The tree stands ahead, mocking me with its tiny dewdrops glistening in the morning sun. It's majestic, I'd give it that. Tall and thick, probably as old as Grandpa. Its trunk clean, slippery, the bark smooth and whitish brown, poking all the way up into a mist of early morning fog that hides its canopy of leaves.

Survivor Girls don't back down from a challenge. I place a foot on the base of the tree and haul myself up so I can wrap an arm around it. I manage to keep hold long enough to swing a leg up and hug it with my other arm. It's awkward and surely not pretty, but nothing an editor can't fix in post-production.

"What is it with you and trees?"

I yelp and fall backwards into a bush, my shorts getting snagged by a jagged thorn, ripping. It's Ronnie and Theo. I bounce up like nothing happened, hiding the damage to my shorts. "Hey, guys! Where are you coming from?"

"Camp," Theo says, waving in the opposite direction from the road. I take a breath of relief. No way they saw the golf cart, then.

"We're looking for firewood," Ronnie says, her arms already filled up with branches and twigs.

"Need help?" I say, picking up a small log.

"You can't burn that!" Theo calls. "There's poison ivy all over it!"

I throw it to the ground. "Good job, Theo!" I call back. "You pass the test on identifying dangerous plants of the swamp."

He looks at me for a moment, then breaks into a grin. "Wow, thanks." He nudges Ronnie. "Survivor Girl just gave me a test and I passed."

"Want to see our camp?" Ronnie asks me.

"Uh . . ." It would be cool to see a real-life archae-ology dig, but—

"You're allowed," Theo says. "The counselors are really cool."

"Come on, we want to show you something." Ronnie hefts a couple of branches from her arms into mine. "It's just a little bit east of here."

I struggle to look at my watch with my arms full and I see it's only eight a.m. Breakfast won't be served for another half hour and taping won't begin until after that. "Is it far?" I ask.

They shake their heads and start marching toward the dense swampy forest.

"I only have a couple of minutes, okay?" I follow them, cracking a dead twig off a tree and adding it to my pile.

Theo gives me a thumbs-up over his shoulder and then holds a pricker bush back for Ronnie and me to pass by, juggling his own armful of firewood. It's pricker bush after pricker bush out here and the trees are closer together, the ground going from wet dirt to mud puddles to little lakes of water we have to walk around. Ronnie and Theo take turns holding the biggest pieces of wood, passing them back and forth while I can barely feel my arms with my wimpy load of twigs.

"Almost there!" Ronnie says, as Theo pulls down a spiderweb with a stick to clear her path. And I wonder if they're boyfriend-girlfriend or just best friends. Most of the boys in my class would push you directly into a spiderweb if they saw one. I trip over a rock, losing half of my kindling.

And then I realize I haven't been paying attention at all to where we're going. "Guys?" I fumble for my compass.

"We're here!" Ronnie tosses her armful of firewood on the ground and collapses on a giant rock.

I push past a pine tree and there's the camp, sleeping bags slung over branches, tents in a row, boots and waders and shovels strewn about. Kids are sitting on little chairs, barely more than a thin cushion keeping them off the swampy ground, eating oatmeal right out of the paper wrapper. My stomach grumbles.

"We have a visitor, everyone," Theo says, and most of the kids look up from their breakfast. "This is Alison Kensington,"—he looks at them all meaningfully—"Survivor Girl."

And it's kind of cool being the celebrity for once because everyone hops up, oatmeals still in their hands, and rushes over, so happy to see me. Like I'm everybody's long-lost best friend. And then there's a thousand questions all at the same time about my dad and making shelters out of bat poop and eating mosquitoes for lunch.

"I've never actually eaten a mosquito," I confess, but then their faces fall, so I add, "for lunch, I mean."

Two adults stride over, also looking at me like I'm the president of the United States or something. "Welcome to Camp Dig," one of them says.

"Hey." I wave like all of this is no big deal. Like I do this all the time.

"We found her climbing a tree," Ronnie tells them. "Can you believe it?"

"I really love climbing trees," I say. "And so many other survivor-ish things."

"What are you doing in the Great Dismal Swamp?" a girl with braids asks.

"Taping a show." I gesture in what I think is the general direction of the set, though at this point I'm totally guessing. "Family fishing trip in the Great Dismal Swamp gone bad. That's the theme."

They think this is the coolest thing they've ever heard and—honestly—I'm getting why Dad loves this so much.

"Will you sign my *Survivor Guy* knife?" A kid whips out his pocketknife, the *Survivor Guy* insignia stamped on the side. One of the counselors hands me a marker and I'm signing knives and bear spray cans and fishing rods for what feels like an hour.

When a kid holds out a dirty undershirt for me to sign, my hand is throbbing and I look at Ronnie. And maybe Harper's not the only person who gets my telepathic signals, because Ronnie jogs over.

"Survivor Girl probably has to get back soon," she says, ushering the kid away, and then she pulls me from the crowd and shows me her tent.

"I bet you'd die for one of these about now," she says, pointing to a tiny sleeping pad rolled out over a muddy tent floor. "Keeps me dry for most of the night." She squeezes her sleeping bag, which is hanging in the sun outside the tent. "See? Almost dry. I don't know how you sleep out in the open like you do."

"Yeah, pretty rough," I say, and I wonder what she would think if I told her I actually slept in a camper.

Would she still want to show me all her stuff? Would she still want to be my friend?

"Even if I keep my tent zipped all day, there's still at least a few critters in here at night. Have to sleep with one eye open, you know?"

I'm horrified for her. "What kind of critters?"

"Mostly bugs. Have you seen those huge beetles yet?"

I wave casually. "Old friends by now."

She shudders, pulling me past the rest of the tents to a tidy cutout of earth surrounded by a string fence, with two kneeling kids leaning over the side, dusting some rocks with a paintbrush.

"This is one of our dig sites. We've found evidence of an ancient fire pit."

"Really? You guys found that?"

"And then over here . . ." She steers me to a huge tree, its roots sprouting out of the ground as thick as little tree trunks holding it up. It looks like the ones we saw growing in Lake Drummond, their long, branch-like roots keeping them above the water. Except we're on dry land now. "This is where Theo and I've been working with one of the group leaders. It may be one of the oldest trees in the swamp, and she thinks it was actually used as a shelter at one time." I peek around one of the roots and see a small space underneath. It's a hideout made from nature.

"Shelter from what?" I ask.

Ronnie shrugs. "Anything dangerous, I guess. Animals, maybe? Or bad swamp conditions? So far we've only found a few animal bones, but she's pretty sure if we keep digging, slowly, we might find evidence of people using this space."

"Like what kind of evidence?"

"Pottery or glass. Really anything that doesn't naturally belong in the dirt." Ronnie bends down and picks up a shovel and some other tools that look more like dental instruments, putting them on a small towel next to the tree. "Anything we find goes to a museum and we get to put our name on it."

"Cool." I'm still looking, disappointed I don't see anything mysterious or out of the ordinary.

"Want to go inside?" Ronnie crawls between two roots. "Come on. I'll put the light on for you."

She flicks on a flashlight sitting on the dirt floor, illuminating the dark space under the tree. Just enough room in there for two people. The flashlight flickers and Ronnie shakes it. "Needs new batteries." She grabs my hand and pulls me inside.

I'm careful to avoid the spot where they've been digging, bordered with string like the larger area outside. I slide a shovel over and sit next to her.

"Do you ever get sick of being a celebrity?" she asks.

I laugh. "My dad is the celebrity. I don't actually sign a lot of autographs normally."

"I'm surprised," she says.

"It's the truth." And, it must be all the talk lately with Jake and Adam about lies and reality, because I wish for a moment I could just tell her. How my dad is just an actor. How I had a doughnut for breakfast yesterday instead of grasshoppers.

"Just imagine the people who sat in here before us," Ronnie says, looking around. "More than a hundred years ago. Cool to think about it, right?"

"How did you get into this?" I ask.

"My dad," she says, shining the light up onto a smooth tree ceiling. "He's an archaeology professor at a university. He also travels, all over the world, to different archaeology sites. He's not home a lot." She looks at me. "He's not a Survivor Guy, but he's kind of famous in his field."

I sigh. "I know what that feels like. When your dad travels a lot."

"I was thinking you would know about that." She smiles, picking up a tool. "But, he got this for me before I left for camp. My first pickaxe. See?" It has her initials engraved on the handle.

"Oh," I say. "Just like me. We're both following in our dad's footsteps." I pat the sides of my shorts, looking for my compass to show her, but I don't feel it. "Wait." I'm on my knees, digging in my pockets. "My compass. I must have dropped it."

Ronnie straightens, directing the light to the ground where I'm sitting, but it's not there. I rush out of the tree. "It's from my dad. I dropped it somewhere."

"Alison?" Theo's there, picking mud off a pail of tools. "Are you okay?"

"My compass." I try to keep my cool with all of the kids watching, but it's hard. Super hard when you've lost your most treasured possession. "It fell out of my pocket!"

And then everyone is searching for me, on hands

and knees, with shovels and brushes. But there is nothing. It's nowhere to be found.

Ronnie and Theo walk me back toward my branchless tree. We go slow and steady, searching the ground. "It's brass," I say. "With scratches all over it."

We walk all the way to the little clearing, no one talking, all three of us sort of panic-searching together. There's nothing at the base of the tree. Nothing in the bog, even though I plunge my arms in to feel around.

"It's from my dad," I say again, standing with them at the base of my tree. "So, it's kind of special."

Ronnie puts her arm around me. "We'll keep looking back at our camp. I know how important it is."

"We're good at finding things," Theo said. "Don't worry."

But I do worry, and I don't tell them the biggest reason I need that compass back. It's because the engraving says FOREVER MY SURVIVOR GIRL. And that's a one-in-a-million promise. A promise I can't lose.

TWENTY

When I get back to the set and park the golf cart, I find everyone out of their tents and campers, walking around with coffees and clipboards and cameras. I scour the ground, hoping that somehow I dropped my compass before I left this morning, ignoring Isabel bouncing beside me. "I lost something," I say. "Go away."

I walk to our trailer and then back to the golf carts again, looking hard for a glint of brass in the sun. My heart throbs in my chest. The compass is nowhere to be found.

Adam and Isabel are looking into Lucy the alligator's pen. I give up my search and stand a few feet behind them.

". . . she's probably not sad," I hear Adam say. "She doesn't know what it's like outside of her cage and sometimes it's easier to live without something when you don't know how good it is."

"She wants to be with the other alligators," Isabel insists.

"You have a big heart for someone who's just a tiny pipsqueak," Adam replies, and then he tickles her, teasing. "And I mean *tiny* pipsqueak. Like the tiniest in the history of tiny."

Isabel tackles him and Adam pretends to get flattened. It's all very annoying, and shouldn't he be helping me climb a tree or something?

"Toddler takedown!" he yells, and then body-slams her as she flails and giggles.

"Ali!" Rick calls to me from one of the walking bridges. He's standing next to a girl who looks my age.

I limp over, having pulled at least one more muscle during my search for the compass.

"Meet Mindy, your stunt double."

I'm so shocked I nearly stumble off the bridge, except that Mindy catches me. With one hand, but whatever.

"Wait! I thought we were going to retry the scene today." I'm offended. Highly, highly offended. Doesn't anybody have any confidence in me?

Rick crosses his arms and clears his throat, then coughs. Obviously he can't think of anything to say.

"I was just practicing, actually." I look at Mindy. "While everyone else was eating their breakfast. And I'm pretty sure I can climb that tree now. No problem."

Rick taps his chin with a finger. Mindy is wearing a Sweet Treat Bake Shop shirt just like mine. Where did they get another one on such short notice? And it's not like it looks better on her or even accentuates her rippled arm muscles or anything. Is she some kind of alien?

She eyes me, pulling her hair up into a ponytail like mine. "I wish I could get my hair to frizz like that." She frowns.

Now that I look closer, I can tell she's not actually twelve. She's practically old. She's had years and years more than me to work on her muscles.

Dad and Jake jog over, Jake already laughing, and I wonder where a good yellow fly is when I need one.

"Welcome! Welcome!" Dad says to Mindy. "Wow,

are those real muscles? Do we have these in the prop store?" She holds out a bicep and Dad gives it a good squeeze, turning to me. "You see these?"

"I thought I was going to climb the tree, Dad."

"Watch this," Rick says. He flicks a wrist toward the closest tree and Mindy scrambles up and waves from one of the branches.

"It was a challenge finding a stunt double that looks twelve, but I did it," he boasts. What does he want? A trophy?

Mindy comes racing back, not even out of breath, bouncing on the balls of her feet like a boxer. "When's the shoot?" She flexes her muscles again. "Do I have time for a quick workout?"

Jake pokes me in the shoulder, grinning.

"Shut up," I mumble, poking him back, hard, and then announcing, "I'm going to breakfast if anyone cares!"

I start off toward the dining tent and nobody tries to stop me. They're all piling into the golf carts to take Muscle Mindy to my bog and my branchless tree so they can ooh and aah over her climbing ability. It makes me sick. They didn't even give me a chance.

The breakfast crew is just starting to clean up

when I get in the omelet line. The ham and cheese omelets are gone, leaving only the veggie omelets: spinach, mushroom, and green peppers. The chef appears and hands me a pop tart. "I've been saving the last one for you. They're just as good the second day."

"Thanks," I say, adding it to my plate and grabbing a chocolate milk box on my way out. I'm going to eat my breakfast in the complete and beautiful quiet of my camper. I'm going to watch a terrible TV show and try to get enough Internet to email Harper and tell her how much I miss her even if she's still mad at me.

But when I step outside the dining tent, Isabel is there, holding a glitter-pink leash. "Want to take Pudding for a walk with us?"

Laura takes the leash away from her. "No kids allowed. Sorry, Isabel."

"Not even a kid that's almost five? Because I'll be five any day now."

The animal trainer smiles at her. "Your birthday isn't for another two months."

Isabel flops onto the ground, tantrum style. "Please! Pleasepleasepleasepleaseplease!"

One of the props guys walks by with a tub full of dead swamp muskies and holds one out to her. "Give me a fish smile!" he says, making the fish talk. I gag at the sight of the dead animals. It's just a reflex I guess, because I'm so kindhearted, but Isabel thinks it's the most hilarious thing she's ever seen.

She stands up. "Can I hold one?" Laura thanks the props guy and hurries away with Pudding's leash.

Isabel reaches into the tub and pulls out a muskie half the size of her body. "Are you sure those are all dead? Because they bite," I say to the props guy.

"I would never let Isabel get hurt," he makes the fish say to me. He turns and tickles her. "Right, Isabel? Right?" She writhes and laughs and drops her fish. Why is everyone constantly tickling this girl and going on and on about how cute she is? Hasn't anyone noticed that she still picks her nose and eats it?

Then, out of the corner of my eye, I see two people coming out of the woods by the fire road. Two people who don't belong on set. Ronnie and Theo.

I drop my plate of breakfast and run, still chewing, across the field to get to them before they can round the corner and see the full set. They can't find out the truth about *Survivor Guy* before I even get the chance to explain it myself. But it's too late. By the time I reach them, their expressions have changed, Theo's neck reddening.

"Hey." It's like I can't breathe, the thick swamp air collecting in my mouth, choking me. "Guys, I——"

"Is this the set?" Theo asks.

They're looking past me, taking it all in, and when I turn around, I see *Survivor Guy* through their eyes. The circus tents and million-dollar campers. The five-man crew building a makeshift raft. Isabel and the props guy. The teatime cart parked by the dining tent. And then the animal trainer walks past us with a giant black mountain lion on a glitter-pink leash.

"I thought you didn't have any shelter?" Ronnie says, looking like she might cry, whatever idea she had of *Survivor Guy*—of me—shattered.

"I know . . ." I begin.

"This is all for *Survivor Guy*?" Theo is getting louder. "You lied?"

"Wait . . ." I back up and run directly into Isabel.

She holds up my pop tart. "You dropped this!" she says. "I dusted it off so you can eat it. Chef's not making any more, you know."

"You have a *chef*?" Ronnie exclaims, and then she throws something at my feet, turns, and runs back into the trees.

Theo gives me a long, hateful look and races after her.

"That was not nice," Isabel says, while I stand there frozen. "You're not supposed to throw things."

She bends over and reaches down. Ronnie and Theo are gone, disappeared into the thickness of the dismal woods.

"What is it?" Isabel asks, turning the compass over.

"Just something my dad gave me."

She shakes it. "Maybe I can play with it sometime?"

When I don't answer, she pokes my side and hands it to me. And even though I've found my most treasured possession, I can't shake the feeling that I've lost something even more important.

TWENTY-ONE

The next day we're supposed to go on a hike to forage edible plants and look for small rodents to kill, even though the prop tent has a thousand stuffed rabbits and plastic rats and possums. I call it the death march, especially since Muscle Mindy is coming in case I can't "keep up the pace."

"Is someone really going to kill an animal?" I ask. "Because if that's the case then I am philosophically against this 'hike,' as you call it."

Muscle Mindy runs up next to me, jogging in place. "I love the smell of swamp in the afternoon." What a totally disgusting thing to say. I walk faster, splashing mud on my boots.

Adam, Jake, and the props guy are up ahead,

whispering about something, so I nose myself between them, nearly tripping over a pricker bush.

Adam peels away from me with a loud sigh, jogging to catch up with Isabel, who's collecting pinecones. He scoops her onto his shoulders and spins her around. "Now, this is the real thing, Isabel. Don't ever forget it." He says this just loudly enough for me to hear, and I know what he's getting at, but I pretend like he doesn't even exist in my world.

We're walking in the general direction of Camp Dig. I can't be sure exactly where it is, but I'm hoping and crossing my fingers that we don't stumble upon it. Or run into Ronnie and Theo scavenging for wood. My stomach aches thinking about what happened and I decide I'm going to avoid them like an infectious disease the rest of my time here. I look over my shoulder and pay special attention to the brush around me.

"Do we have to take all this stuff off for the scene?" I say to the group. We're wearing matching sweatshirts that say YOU'VE BEEN SURVIIIIIIIVED! on the backs, our hoods pulled over our heads, cinched up tight to protect us from the yellow flies. It's about a hundred million degrees, and sweat is dripping into my eyes, but at least we're not getting bitten. Jake has on the bug-net helmet that Betsy Sue's kid died in, but the rest of our faces are exposed. The gnats are awful, flying into my nose and mouth and swarming around my eyes. "Aren't you worried you'll get bit?" I ask Jake.

He waves toward Claire, who's laughing at something Dad said, leaning her cheek on his shoulder. "She's got my EpiPen. I'll only have my gear off for a few minutes anyway."

I look around, fanning the gnats from my face, worrying that it will only take a minute for the yellow flies to find Jake. They are the worst in the woods, especially in the afternoon. And then what? We're at least a twenty-minute hike from the set.

"When are they making the official announcement?" props guy asks, adjusting his heavy backpack.

"What announcement?" I say, pumping my sweatshirt in and out for some air. "I keep hearing about this."

Adam turns around and gives Jake a look, Isabel still on his shoulders.

"What?" I ask.

"Talk to Dad," Jake says, and so I do, backpedaling past Muscle Mindy doing squats and Bianca polishing her lens, inserting myself directly between Claire and my dad.

"We were just talking about you!" Claire says. "Isabel absolutely loves you, Ali."

I ignore her. "Jake says there's going to be an announcement, Dad?"

Dad and Claire exchange not-so-secret eye signals, making my face burn fire.

"Am I the only one who doesn't know about this?"

Rick, who's been leading the group, stops at the edge of what looks like a drop-off and turns around to face us. "Okay, let's start rolling."

Bianca jogs past us, her camera poised and ready, Wes trotting along beside her.

"Let's talk about it in a little bit," Dad whispers, taking his sweatshirt off. But I can already feel myself getting jittery-upset.

"Did you add another shoot after this?" I say, because this is supposed to be the last episode of the season. And then he's coming home so we can be a family and all the puzzle pieces will be in the right place.

Rick claps once. "Okay, maybe some foraging

or hunting and gathering could happen right about now?"

We take off our protective layers, and the sweltering swamp air feels cool for a second on my sweaty skin. Claire stands next to Jake, holding his EpiPen and his bug helmet.

Dad kisses me on the forehead. "Let's find some food for tonight and then we'll talk."

Wes captures the whole thing on audio, standing way too close all of a sudden. I pull my ponytail tighter, hitting him right in his boom mic. Accidentally on purpose.

Jake holds up a dead squirrel. "Would this work for dinner, Dad?"

"Did you just kill that thing?" I ask, horrified, but then I see the props guy behind a tree, zipping up his backpack.

"Yep. Bare handed."

When I get closer, I see it's only a stuffed animal.

"Great job, son," Dad says. "How about a few of these guys on the side?" He holds out his hands, revealing a swirling mass of earthworms.

I gag. I can't help it.

"FACT! Earthworms are easy to find in a survival

situation and provide protein and nutrients vital for the human body." He holds one up like he's going to eat it. "They taste good too."

And then he laughs, breaking Survivor Guy character. "Did you think I was going to do it?" He slaps his knee, handing the worms back to the props guy.

Rick is standing at the drop-off now, looking over the edge. "George. Come and take a look at this gully. What if crossing this is the only way back to camp?"

Dad inspects the ravine, looking at Jake and me, waving us over. Bianca falls in step with us, Wes fastening little wireless mics onto our shirts.

"I could jump this no problem," Jake says, pushing his chest out. "I did the long jump in track that one year, remember?"

"It's narrow and pretty dry." Dad looks at me. "What do you think, Ali?"

In all reality, this so-called gully isn't as narrow as I'd like, not to mention it's deeper than the deep end of our pool, but I feel the camera on me, feel the weight of the mic on my chest. "Yeah, sure. No problem for me either."

Dad turns to the camera, his voice deepening with urgency. "It's getting late. We're vulnerable out here in the wilderness full of flies and snakes and panthers. We've come far only to find we can't go any farther. Not unless"—he looks pointedly at the trench— "we jump."

"Dad." Jake stands next to him, hands on his hips. "Let me go first. To test the danger."

I roll my eyes. "Yeah, let him go first, Dad."

Muscle Mindy stops her leg squats and calls to me, "Want me to take this one for you, Amy?"

"It's Ali," I say. "And no. Thanks."

Rick is peering into the ditch. "Hey, is that a snapping turtle?"

Dad bends down for a closer look. "Yep." He kneels at the edge, pulling out a pair of binoculars. "Yep, yep, yep. You don't want to fall in there."

"Great," I say.

Adam snickers beside me. "One hundred percent there's no turtle."

I cross my arms, looking down into the deep gully just as Jake shouts, "Now, that's a big snapping turtle!"

I don't tell him, but Adam's right. The ravine is empty except for mud and rocks and leaves.

Dad speaks into the camera. "Snapping turtle.

Indigenous to this area. Vicious and territorial. One slip and—FACT!—you *will* get bitten."

"I'm going," Jake says, coiling up to jump. "We need to get across." And then he leaps, legs stretched, coming down into a body roll on the other side.

Dad stands up, patting me on the shoulder. "There's only one way out of this swamp, Ali," he says. "You've got to get over this gully." And then he gestures behind me, and Muscle Mindy bounces over. The makeup lady rushes out, dabbing some redness onto her chin to look like pimples, which I don't appreciate.

"Wait," I say. "I want to do this part."

Everyone freezes and Bianca lowers her camera.

"No," Rick says. "This is why we got you a stunt double."

I groan, because now more than ever I want to do this shot. I don't want to play a Survivor Girl on camera anymore. I want to *be* Survivor Girl. "Dad."

"Sweetheart," Dad says. "We want you to look like your best Survivor Girl on camera, remember? Girl power?"

"Let her do it," Adam says, stepping in front of his dad. "Just let her try it."

Rick shakes his head, looking sternly at Adam. "She's going to hurt herself. This is why I'm the producer. I make these decisions, not you."

Adam stalks off, mumbling about how none of this matters anyway.

"You took away my tree climb," I say, breaking the awkward silence. "I can do this, Dad."

Muscle Mindy is clearly annoyed, sighing and grunting and hopping from foot to foot, warming up.

"George?" Rick says, and I see him glance over his shoulder at Adam, that same look in his eyes from before that makes me ache inside. "She's your daughter, you make the call. I'm not always right."

"One chance, Ali," Dad says, Claire patting him on the back. "And let's get going. We've got to get through this."

Rick nods his head in agreement and then everyone moves aside and I get my chance. With about ten pairs of eyes watching, all expecting me to fail. And, honestly, we all know jumping and leaping are not my strongest survivor skills. But I'm not letting some old lady play me on camera whenever something gets tough. I have dignity, you know.

The gully is wider than I thought, and I size up the gap in my mind. Even if I splash-landed in the muddy water, I could run up the other end, narrowly missing the pretend snapping turtle. That would make for good TV, right? I ignore Mindy breathing behind me. I count to three and then run, my legs pumping, gaining speed, and—jump. Leap. Soar. I'm a ballerina instead of a mediocre archer playing a survivalist on a TV show. And I almost make it. I touch the other side with the tip of my shoes, but the tiny bit of land beneath them gives way, falling into the gully below, and I follow hard and fast. I land crumpled against the side of the ditch and it's slippery and mud-soaked, sending me sliding and rolling into the little bit of water, where I land head-first on the pointed edge of a rock.

I know I'm hurt when I see Bianca dump her camera on the ground and slide in after me, followed by Adam and Jake and Claire. "Nobody touch her!" Claire yells.

My arm is bent under my body and the rock is hard and cold on my skin. "Dad?"

Claire is there, touching me lightly on my forehead, helping me sit up, and I can hear the sound of something like sobbing, and I think it's me. And I wish it wasn't.

How did I think I could ever be a real Survivor Girl? It's like I was lying even to myself.

There's a golf cart, and somehow I'm in it and we're driving slowly back to the set and I take out my compass and hold it and ignore the blood on my hand and on the towel Claire keeps folding over and placing back onto my head. I pretend I'm on a bouncy school bus heading home, with Harper sitting next to me, and she's not mad anymore and we're sneaking gummy bears and laughing at our own bad jokes.

I pretend that for a long time, and Harper tells me it's not too bad and holds my hand and maybe it's weird that it's not my mom's hand I dream about. Then a headache, sharp as the rock, pulls me out of my pretending and I'm sweating on a cot in the medical tent, a fan blowing directly onto my body. Jake and Dad are hovering in the doorway, whispering to Claire. I sit up, an ice pack falling into my lap. "Ouch." My forehead is thumping and when I touch it, there's a giant bandage.

Dad hurries over and sits on the end of the cot.

"Scared me back there, Ali." He's inspecting my head. "Cut yourself pretty good, right on your forehead."

"You missed dinner," Jake adds. "And also dessert. Ice cream. Want me to get you one?"

I try to shake my head but it hurts too much, and I see through the opening in the tent that the sun is low over the lake now. Almost sunset.

"Claire says you might have a concussion," Dad says. "I'd like you to sleep here tonight."

"What? No, I'm fine, Dad. I just need my own bed." I don't look at Claire. "My camper bed, I mean."

Dad straightens the sheets. "Claire's real good at taking care of people. I don't know what to do for concussions, Ali."

"Dad."

He's standing up though and stretching. "We've got a nighttime scene to shoot and then I'll come back and check in on you, okay?"

I pull myself out of bed, teetering on tingly legs. "What about me? Shouldn't I be in the scene?"

Isabel tiptoes in from outside, her face a mess of chocolate sauce and sprinkles. "Mom?" But then she sees me and rockets over, giving me a chocolaty hug. I flop back onto my bed and Claire pulls her off me.

"If I'm so injured, maybe I should go to a real hospital." I cross my arms, this time looking hard at Claire. Because for all I know, she's just an actress too. With so much fakeness all around, how am I supposed to know what's real?

"Ali." Claire puts the ice pack on my bed, ushering Isabel to her hammock area. "You need to stay here. With me, okay?" Like all of a sudden she's my mom or something.

"She's sleeping here with us?" Isabel shouts, throwing her stuffed animals into the air. "Like a sleepover?"

Dad kisses me on the forehead and Jake punches me in the shoulder, and then they leave and I'm choking on the awkwardness of it all.

Even though the air is thick with swamp in this tent, I pull the covers over my head and close my eyes, pretending I'm in my own bed at home, far away from this place. I ignore Isabel's little-girl sounds while she plays with her dolls and gets ready for bed with her mom, singing the brush-your-teeth song. I pretend I'm sleeping when Dad comes back and reads *Where the Wild Things Are* to Isabel, now tucked in her hammock. I don't listen when Max in the book is being really awful. Or when he makes it to the island. Or when Isabel wants to know if there are wild things living in the Great Dismal Swamp. I don't even get up when Claire brings me some dinner, set aside just for me from the chef, and leaves it next to my hospital cot.

Where the Wilds Things Are used to be our story, mine and Jake's and Dad's, before things got complicated. Dad read it so much, we could all recite it from memory together.

I wonder if Dad even remembers.

TWENTY-TWO

Everything hurts when I get out of bed the next morning. It's not just my head anymore. But I lie when Claire asks me how I feel.

"Great." I stretch and bend over to get my shoes, a searing pain rocketing up my leg. She hands me some medicine and a bottle of water, shaking her head.

"You're just like your father, you know. God forbid a Kensington has a real injury that requires some bed rest." She snorts. "I want you to take it easy. You've got a nasty cut on your forehead that I had to glue shut, and a minor concussion." She looks at me. "That's no joke, okay?"

I take the medicine when she's not looking.

Muscle Mindy is running circles around the medical tent with Isabel on her back when I step out into the sun.

"Hey, Amy!" she says, trotting past, and I don't even correct her.

I hear Dad's voice coming from the prop tent and I take my time walking over, still feeling a bit wobbly. He's rummaging through the bin of fishing gear with the props guy when I step through the flap door. On one side of the tent is a long table divided into little squares with masking tape, one for each prop item. The stuffed squirrel is there, its little square labeled SQUIRREL, SCENE 7, DAY 4. There are a lot of random things, like a fishing net, a plastic gray mouse, bear spray, a *Survivor Guy* knife, three pieces of firewood, a snakeskin, the hook made out of a rock, and a cluster of dead yellow flies. The other side of the tent is a mess of stacked boxes filled with junk. The one next to me is overflowing with paper leaves of every color.

"Hey, Dad," I say. "I'm back. Ready for another day on set."

He rushes over and gives me a delicate hug, then

looks at my head. "Does it hurt? Does Claire know you're out of bed?"

"Just a tiny concussion. I'm fine."

They let me back on the set for the day, but Claire and Muscle Mindy follow my every step. The makeup lady spends a long time fashioning a paper leaf bandage to go over my real one. Muscle Mindy gets one to match and basically does the entire morning shoot for me, except for the parts where Dad's cooking up a swamp muskie for lunch while Jake and I are sitting on the beach of the lake. When there's absolutely no potential risk of bodily harm.

The rest of the time, I sit on a camping chair a few feet away, under an umbrella for shade. Adam sits next to me and we watch Muscle Mindy fake-build a raft with my brother and Dad. I can't even look at him. He stuck up for me at the ditch, and I blew it.

Rick interrupts the raft-building. "Mindy, maybe a little less grunting? We're hoping to emphasize the strengthening father-son and -daughter relationships, not muscles."

Adam crosses his arms and shakes his head. "I can't wait to leave this place."

I touch my head delicately, my injury throbbing

under the bandage. "Why do you fight with him so much?" They've been at each other's throats all morning. And I'm pretty sure it's my fault. "You didn't have to stick up for me, you know."

Adam skips a stone across the lake. "I'm only here because my mom said I have to be. He's not my real dad."

"What?" I say. "Really?"

Adam sighs, tossing a pinecone into the water. "No. I mean, my stepdad is my real dad. Not him."

I try to skip a stone across the chocolate lake water, but it just sinks out of sight.

"My stepdad never left me and my mom for some stupid show."

A sharp pain shoots through my forehead. "He left you?"

"Four years ago."

It's when *Survivor Guy* started to get popular. I was eight when Dad started disappearing for weeks at a time for tapings. But he always came back.

"It's like all of a sudden this guy I don't know anymore wants me to hang out with him again. Like that's going to make everything better."

I wonder if his parents were fighting all the time

and pretending they weren't. I want to ask him if his dad ever stayed in hotels instead of coming home and sleeping in his own house. I wonder so many things, but then the raft-building scene is over and I don't ask any of my questions. Because maybe I don't want to know.

Everyone breaks for afternoon tea and I'm so tired and headachy and body-throbbing, I skip it and go take a nap in the camper.

When I wake up, it's dark outside and I'm discombobulated. Did I miss dinner? Where is everyone? The set is empty and the dining tent is dark. The moon is full, casting shadows across the swampy ground. I step outside, looking for Dad and Jake. I see light pouring out of the cottage with the big screened porch, and what must be the entire crew crowded together inside.

"You're going to miss it." Laura comes trotting up, pulling off the gloves she uses to feed the animals. "It's about to start."

"What is?" I ask, but then I know. The announcement.

The animal trainer and I squeeze inside. Dad's standing next to the fireplace while Rick is perched on the hearth talking to the crew about how to survive quicksand. Dad's stunt double and Muscle Mindy are each roasting six marshmallows at once on long sticks, passing them back when they're browned. They've got all the dangerous jobs. I push through the crowd, and when Mindy waggles one in front of my face, I can't help myself. I take it.

"Okay!" Rick claps and whistles until the crowd quiets. "I'd like to turn it over to the man himself, the real-life Survivor Guy who not only outsmarted a sea of hungry sharks as a young boy, but managed to convince the wildlife service that manages the Great Dismal Swamp to host our crew for this production. George Kensington!"

Rick sweeps an arm in Dad's direction and pulls him up onto the hearth, jiggling his shoulders and knocking him in the head like they're best buddies.

Jake comes up beside me. "Big news, Ali!"

My mouth is full of marshmallow and I grunt, "Will someone please tell me what's going on?"

Rick is standing off to the side now, holding a rope attached to a banner or something that's rolled up above the fireplace mantel.

Dad clears his throat and I attempt to wipe the

sticky marshmallow from my hands, but just manage to spread the mess to my shirt. I fantasize that Dad's about to announce he's taking a break from *Survivor Guy* to come home and be with his family for a while. *Survivor Guy*'s success may have meant we got a new pool, but Dad hasn't even been home long enough to swim in it. And what's more important than family, right?

"Good evening, crew!" Everyone claps until Dad raises his hand for them to stop. "I hope everyone's planning on a nice soak in the hot tub tonight for those sore muscles." He winks and everyone roars with laughter. "But, seriously, a lot of magic's been happening this week." He points to a man in a *Survivor Guy* safari hat by the door and then to the chef standing next to him. "Daniel caught a bluespotted sunfish with a fishing spear, and Lou made a fantastic pot roast for dinner." He looks to the other side of the room. "Bianca taped some amazing footage at the lake today, and Samuel made a snorkel out of a hollowed twig."

Everyone claps, the chef takes a bow, and Bianca waves, a camera not hefted to her shoulder for once.

"We've come a long way since our web series days," Dad continues. "Getting picked up by a network made us the top-rated survival show, leaving *Me in the Wild* in the dust and"—Dad has to talk louder over the hoots and hollers—"last week I signed a new contract"—the crew erupts in cheers again—"for another fifteen episodes."

Jake grabs my hand and squeezes it. "When?" I say to him, pulling out of his grip. "When does the next season start? He's coming home first, right?"

"But a few changes are going to happen," Dad says. The room falls completely silent and I can hear the bugs singing in the swamp. There must be a billion of them.

Rick pulls the rope and the banner tumbles open, revealing the words SURVIVOR GUY AND SON: THE NEW GENERATION, MONDAYS AT 7 P.M. in giant skyscraper-size red letters. Jake is jumping up and down like he's at a concert, bumping me with his elbow. Survivor Guy *and Son*?

"That's not all," Dad says. "Most of you know this already, but for those who don't—"

Rick pulls the rope again and a second banner

unfurls, this one with a black and white drawing of a fancy triangle building with a SURVIVOR GUY, INC. sign on the front of it. At the bottom, it says SAN DIEGO, CA.

"I'm moving to San Diego!" Jake yells in my face. "And I'm going to be Survivor Son!"

"What?" I say. "We're moving?" And nobody asks me? What about Harper? And archery? I'm supposed to just leave everything behind and start over again? Does anyone know what that could do to a teenage girl?

Somehow everything is so loud all at once, I'm suffocating. Champagne is being passed over my head, dripping onto me. And then everyone's singing the *Survivor Guy* jingle so loudly I can't hear the bugs anymore.

"Dad says you can join us when you turn eighteen too!" Jake says. "It will be a whole *Survivor Guy* family thing!"

I feel sick, dizzy, the room too hot and full. Because I realize that we're not moving. Just Dad and Jake. He's splitting up the family. He's leaving me and Mom.

Dad spots me from his perch on the fireplace, his

smile dropping. When was he planning on telling me? He jumps into the crowd, coming for me, but I wedge myself backwards past the crew clinking their glasses with their life-is-perfect smiles. I push past Muscle Mindy and the chef and the guy that speared a fish. And then Adam's there, looking at me sad and sorry like I'm a two-year-old who just dropped her Popsicle in the sand. I swing away from him, out the door. Dad calls my name, but I keep walking, hoping I can find a patch of quicksand to swallow me up whole.

TWENTY-THREE

When Dad and Jake get back to the trailer, I'm trying to sleep, wishing the thin curtain between me and the rest of the world was a hundred-pound door with a thousand bolt locks. I shut my eyes tight and keep them closed, even when I feel the curtain open and hear someone breathing into my space. It's Dad. He touches my ear and I pretend I'm in a coma.

"Ali-Gator." He nudges my shoulder. One, two, three times.

When he gives up, I feel the whoosh of the curtain closing. I open my eyes and turn over to look out the window at the swamp.

Dad and Jake are talking about their big move in the kitchen area. Jake wants to know if he can bring girls to the *Survivor Guy* set. Dad only wants to talk about the Pacific Islands.

"FACT!" Dad says. "They actually have flying fish there. And sea turtles like you wouldn't believe. You ever swim with a dolphin?"

I hear cabinets thumping closed. Snacks being opened and ice cubes in glasses. They're still celebrating. Without me.

It's windy outside and I watch as a paper coffee cup tumbles past my window. I can see the back side of the leaves and the trees bending with the force of each gust.

"How're we going to get my bed to San Diego?" Jake asks.

I picture Jake's room empty and my stomach tightens. How could Dad split up the family like this? I always thought the separation was Mom's fault, because of her bad moods when Dad was around, rolling her eyes when she thought I wasn't looking, never letting anyone forget when Dad was late or missing something important. But—maybe I was wrong all this time. She must have known that Dad was leaving us. And maybe that's what she meant when she said I wasn't ready for the set. That I couldn't handle this. She wasn't trying to control me. She really was trying to protect me.

I stare out at the wind-whipped trees, wishing that my phone had one second of service, just one bar, just enough so I could call my mom to come get me. But I must have fallen asleep, because the next thing I know, I'm opening my eyes and everything is dark in the trailer, and the rain hitting our roof sounds like golf balls of hail. Outside, the set is deserted, and small limbs have cracked off the trees and littered the ground. A bolt of lightning illuminates everything for a second and I see the trees are dancing and I can't believe there are any leaves left on them at all with this much wind. I can feel it against the trailer, trying to push us to the swamp water, and I grip my mattress. I peek under the curtain and hang upside down into Jake's bunk.

"Just a storm," he says, half asleep.

There's another explosion of thunder and lightning and I flip back up. The trailer sways, the wind sounding like a truck stuck in the sand. I open my tiny window and let it in. It's moist, earthy, and smoky. Suddenly nobody is in bed anymore, the set coming alive with headlamps. They're converging on the dining tent, which is about to collapse, its stakes flailing in the wind. "Jake?" But when I peek into his bunk, he's out cold. How can anybody sleep through this?

"Dad?" I call, but then I see that the crew has it under control and I feel the pull of sleep on my bruised body. I close my eyes for a minute, and the shouts from set and the sounds of the storm on the swamp mingle with my dream of Harper and pop tarts and alligators in cages.

I don't know what time it is when I open my eyes again, but the set is empty and the very reddish tip of the sun is peeking through the trees. I struggle to shut my window. The air is so much cooler, now that the storm went through. The dining tent is upright again, a dozen more stakes than before securing it in place. My stomach aches from only having a marshmallow for dinner. And then I remember Dad's big announcement and wonder what Harper will think when she sees it on the news today. Probably that I never tell her anything. That I'm keeping secrets. Maybe even lying to her. And the bad thing is, she's mostly right.

There's a light on in the back of the dining tent

and my stomach squinches up with hunger. I open my curtain and launch myself from my top bunk onto the floor. Jake doesn't move. He's still covered in fly bites from the first day. How will he ever be Survivor Son if he can't even take a fly bite? Grandpa once got stung fifteen times by a hornet and still managed to kill it and eat it for dinner, as he described in chapter sixteen, "Bugs, Protein, and You."

I'm going home. I'll stay with Harper until Mom comes back. I just can't be here anymore where my dad has his own little girl to drive his golf carts and play horsey with. And where everything is staged and scripted and fake. I'm such an idiot for believing he was the real thing when everyone else knew the truth. I guess I know him about as much as he knows me. I belong with Mom, where no one will expect me to climb branchless trees or leap over bogs. Where the crowded halls of middle school will be the closest I get to surviving in the wild. Where I'll never have to worry that she'll leave me for someplace with fancy flying fish.

I put a sweatshirt over my muddy Sweet Treat Bake Shop shirt and zip my bag closed, tossing it onto my bunk. Hopefully someone can take me on a boat back to the inlet. Call me a cab. I'll even take a bus. And as soon as I have service again, I'll call Mom.

I won't try to say goodbye to Ronnie and Theo. Or get to explain myself or say sorry. They'll just remember me as some selfish girl that lies to people's faces.

The camper is still dark, Dad sleeping in his room, his snores penetrating his closed door. I look out the window, my stomach growling again, and decide there's time for one more walk.

When I come out of the camper and cross the little bridge to the dining tent, the wind is whipping with the scent of evergreens and—I pause, because again, I smell smoke, and I wonder where it's coming from.

"Hello?" I say when I step inside.

"Breakfast's at seven," the chef calls from behind the privacy screen that separates the kitchen from the dining area, steam coiling overtop.

"Need help?" I ask, taking the closest seat, weak from the walk over on such an empty belly. I mean, how long does it take to succumb to malnourishment? Two hours? Twelve?

The chef comes around the screen, wiping his

hands on a towel, a crackling walkie-talkie hanging from his apron. "Hey!" he says when he sees me, rushing over. "I never told you how worried I was when I heard what happened the other day. Pretty brave of you to take that jump, you know."

I smile. "Or stupid, I guess."

"Risk taker. Just like your dad." He pulls the walkie-talkie off his apron and brings it to his ear, listening to a fuzzy voice. He holds up a just-a-minute finger to me.

I breathe in the sugar-sweet smells filling the tent, but then I snap to attention when I hear something on the radio.

"Did he just say wildfire?"

Chef hangs his walkie-talkie back on his apron. "I've been listening to the emergency alert channel since the storm came through. There was a small fire on the other side of the lake, but it's mostly contained already. Lightning strike."

"But not all the way contained?"

He waves me off with a laugh. "They deal with this all the time, I'm sure." He bustles back to his kitchen and returns with two steaming bowls in his hands, putting one onto the table in front of me. I take a drippy bite of something hot and soupy. I gag. My body just rejects bad food.

"Not a fan of grits?" His radio squawks as he walks back to his kitchen, but I can't make out the words.

"Uh, no, I love it," I call after him, attempting another bite. But I'm distracted, listening to the wind outside, wondering what "mostly contained" means. A plop of grits lands on my bare leg.

"Chef?" He's coming back to the table with honey and brown sugar and butter, lining them up in front of me. "Shouldn't we be worried? About the fire?"

He pats me on the head. "They've probably put it out by now." He sits next to me, diving into his own bowl of grits. "I've got bear claws in the oven, but they need another fifteen minutes."

I stare at him.

"The pastry," he says. "In honor of the bear tracks scene later this morning."

I smile, being polite, because by then I'll be on a bus home. I wonder if they'll have to kill off my character to explain why I'm gone. Maybe they find my scattered clothes near the bear den and assume I've met a grisly end, just like Betsy Sue's son.

A splintering sound crackles through the air, and even though I've never heard it before, I know for sure it's a tree falling. And not just any tree, by the sound of it. A big one. The chef and I leap up, circling each other, not sure where to run. It sounds like it's right over us and it's going to demolish the tent. I've never read anything about surviving a tree fall, so I just hightail it toward the door, because maybe if I can see the tree, I can dodge it. I'm halfway there, the chef gripping me by the forearm, when we hear the tree smash to the ground, and the sound of something exploding in its wake.

Leaves and debris blow in, knocking over a chair by the door. And then there's shouting and hordes of crew members running past. We climb over a tree branch to get out, and then I see it. A mammoth tree smacked down directly onto our camper, splitting it in half.

TWENTY-FOUR

For a moment Chef and I are frozen, until the dangling air-conditioning unit on the camper breaks and falls into the wreckage. I snap out of it and we run to the rubble. The rest of the crew is climbing into the camper where the wall and the back door used to be. Where Dad's bed should be. Chef has a grip on my arm again. "Best stay here, Alison."

Out of the emergency hatch climbs Jake, shirtless and in his boxers, but intact. "Jake!" I pull away from the chef and run toward him, but I'm cut off by the ten or more crew members converging on him as Claire sprints out of the medical tent screaming proper first-aid procedures. The wall-less side of the camper is a flurry of people throwing debris onto the grass, as a plume of dust settles around it.

With each second that Dad and his grinning face don't appear, my composure disintegrates. I pull the compass out of my pocket and rub the surface. Jake tries to climb back into the camper when he doesn't see Dad outside, but Adam is right there with Rick, and they're pulling him away. They sit Jake down on a couch cushion someone tossed onto the ground and he does the "zip-a-dee-doo-dah" whistle over and over again, waiting for Dad to respond. I'm sinking farther into the swamp, the air thickening, the buzz of the bugs getting louder and louder. Rub. Rub. Rub.

"I'm scared." It's Isabel, still in her horsey pajamas. She must have just stumbled out of her hammock. "Where's Mama?" She reaches for my hand but I pull away, pacing.

I face into the wind, begging the universe for my father's safe return, and that's when I see the smoke across the lake. It doesn't look like much from so far away, almost like someone's campfire, but it means that the fire hasn't been put out. Not yet.

Isabel tugs my shirt and I realize suddenly that nobody is throwing debris out of the camper anymore and it's like the whole set is holding its breath. I freeze for a second time. They found him.

Jake stands up, pushing away Claire, who's trying to fasten a bandage to his wrist. We're all staring at the demolished camper and I think this is my fault. It's payback for all my mean thoughts and moping around and hating all the fakeness. How could I be so selfish? It's Hollywood. A TV show. He's trying to make a good life for me, and I don't even appreciate it.

Then the half-hinged door busts open and there stands Dad, dirty and bleeding from a scratch on his face, his pajamas ripped, and missing a sock. But his face is alight with his signature grin. The rest of the crew climbs out the wall-less side of the camper and everyone breaks out in claps and whistles and zip-a-dee-doo-dahs.

"Survivor Guy surviiiives!" he calls out, and Jake and I run to him like we're three years old and he's coming home from work with presents and ice cream cones. And I feel nothing but love and happiness, and I'm never leaving this place without my dad.

"How did you—I mean—that tree fell right on your bed," I say, as we're all still hugging.

Bianca is in our faces now, red light blinking, and

Dad stands straighter. "Instincts, daughter," he says. "Pure survival instincts."

I tug off my sweatshirt, realizing I'm sweltering now that the sun is all the way up. "Dad, your cheek!"

"I'm fine, Dad. Don't worry," Jake interjects.

"Tree branch," Dad says, moving closer to the camera. "Massive deadly tree branch nearly sliced me right through."

Claire is with us now, Isabel on her hip, and she hands her to Dad, breaking up our family hug. Isabel latches onto him with a death grip. And all of a sudden Claire, Isabel, and Dad are in one big sniffly hug and the tingling in my body from relief at seeing him alive and well fades and settles into my stomach like a wad of stale gum.

The camera is in my face. "Thoughts? Reactions?" Bianca gives me a thumbs-up and all I can do is watch Dad console Isabel, who is scared by the trickle of blood on his cheek.

"Perfect." Bianca pats me on the back and moves on to Jake.

The crowd is breaking up, heading toward the dining tent and the sweet smell of bear claws. Punching Dad in the arm as they pass. Rick plants a big wet kiss right on his forehead, and the animal trainer gives him a high-five with an attack glove. Claire puts the procession of fist-bumps and hugs to a stop. "Go on to breakfast, people," she says. "He needs something on this wound." She leads him by the hand toward the hospital tent with Isabel, who is clearly old enough to walk on her own, still attached and hanging from his neck.

"Wait for me!" I say.

"Alison, do you mind watching Isabel for a sec?" Claire asks, peeling her off Dad's shoulders and plopping her on the ground in front of me.

"Actually—"

"Take her to breakfast, maybe?" Claire grabs Dad by the elbow and pulls him closer. "But no fruit punch, okay?"

"I love breakfast," Isabel says.

"Why don't you marry it then?" I reply, like I'm in kindergarten again. Because I'm getting sick and tired of Isabel loving everything all the time.

But she just bursts out laughing, loud and hooting, and all I can do is watch Claire and my dad hold hands as they walk together to the medical tent.

TWENTY-FIVE

Jake sits with Isabel and me at a table, where the breakfast atmosphere is cheerier than it's ever been. Like everyone is celebrating after such a close call with disaster, clinking coffee cups, laughing, being too loud for so early in the morning.

Isabel talks nonstop about the tree. She wants to have another sleepover now that my bed in the camper has been demolished.

"I can move all my animals and you can sleep in my hammock."

"Yeah, where are we going to sleep tonight?" I say to Jake, ignoring Isabel as she eats her bear claw icing-first.

"There are extra beds in some of the trailers," Jake says, shrugging like it's no big deal.

I scarf down my own bear claw, which is admittedly pretty good and also looks kind of like the real thing.

"I know!" I say. "How about we just go home? There's a wildfire in the swamp, in case anyone cares."

"Fire?" Isabel asks, sticky-faced.

Jake shakes his head. "They already put that out."

I look over his shoulder at the lake through the canvas tent window. He's wrong. The pillar of smoke is still there. Is it bigger?

"The swamp is ripe for a peat fire," Adam says, sliding into the seat beside me. "The burning goes underground. No flames."

I take another bite of pastry, but it's not tasting so good anymore.

"Well, we won't be home for a while." Jake steals a strawberry off my plate. "The next season starts in three weeks and there's a ton to prepare."

"I've never heard of a peat fire before," I say, worrying. "And I've read a lot of survivor books." But the air feels different somehow, charged, like that time when there was a tornado watch at Grandma's, where there's no basement to seek shelter.

Adam hasn't touched his oatmeal, and the brown sugar on top is turning into a dark pool. "You should look it up. It's no joke."

"Anyway, Dad promised me he was coming home after this for a while," I tell Jake.

"When?" he mumbles through a mouthful of bear claw. "Because there's no time. We already booked our flights out to Cali."

I drop my fork. "First, nobody tells me that my own dad is moving across the country, and now he's not even coming home first like he promised?" I push my plate away, my voice getting too loud. "How are we supposed to be a family like that?"

"Ali," Jake says. "I tried to say something. You just never want to hear about things like this."

I'm searing mad. My head is pounding so hard, I touch my bandage to make sure it's still there.

"My mom and I are going home," Isabel says. "To our new house, and I'm going to kindergarten." She licks her fingers.

Jake shakes his head, gulping down some orange juice. "You guys are coming with us."

"What?" I stand up. "They're going to California and Mom and I aren't?"

Isabel puts down her bear claw. "You're lying."

"No, I'm not," Jake says.

She pushes her chair back. "I'm telling my mom on you!" And she marches out of the tent with her little hands pulled into fists.

"You're ruining everyone's lives with this. I hope you're happy." I storm out after Isabel, leaving the boys to the rest of their breakfasts.

When I get to the medical tent, Dad's sitting on my hospital cot, a Band-Aid on his cheek. "What happened?" he says sternly, like Isabel's tantrum is my fault. I can hear her in the back room, and let me tell you, that girl can throw a fit.

"George." Claire peeks her head around the hanging towels used as a room divider. "I need you."

Dad stands up, stretching, and walks to the back with me right on his heels. Isabel is a tiny ball on the floor in the middle of a pile of stuffed animals. Curled up so tight no one can get in. She's an armadillo. Claire sits next to her, rubbing her back. "This is an opportunity for us, sweetie. We can't pass it up."

Isabel balls up tighter, her sniffles muffled by her

animals, and for some reason my heart throbs along with my head. Because I know what it feels like when promises are broken. When the pieces in your puzzle aren't fitting together.

"We're going to get you a teacher," Claire says. "George—tell her about the teacher."

Dad sits on the other side of Isabel, stroking her hair. "Just for you. A special kindergarten teacher who's going to come to the set every day just to teach our Isabel."

It's not enough. Isabel doesn't even lift her head. And as my dad and Claire sit there on top of a thousand stuffed animals, patting Isabel on the back, I can tell they know it too.

There's no filming that morning, or even after lunch. The crew is busy removing the giant tree from our camper. I try to go in a few times to see if my phone survived or to at least rescue the General's book from under my pillow, but they're not having it. I walk the shore of the lake with Adam, who is watching the smoke on the other side.

"Wildfires can move fifteen miles per hour," he says. "We should leave."

"Don't you think the park police would tell us

to leave if we were in trouble?" I glance behind me. "What about all of this stuff?" The camper trailers, the tents, the golf carts and tanks of drinking water. The animals.

"You sound like our dads," he says, and for a minute the wind picks up and the smell of smoke is overpowering, making me stand straighter.

The rest of the crew smells it as well, pausing over what they're doing to glance across the lake.

"My dad is moving too, if it makes you feel any better," Adam adds, throwing a rock into the chocolate water.

"Why would that make me feel better?" A weight settles into my gut. "It's fine; I don't even care anymore." I picture Mom and me sitting in our empty house. Jake's bedroom door closed. Dad's stuff all the way moved out from the garage. Everything would be so quiet, and I hate all-the-time quiet.

"You get used to it," Adam says. "Not having your dad around. It's not so bad after a while."

"He's always going to come back," I reply, my eyes getting hot.

"That's what they always say."

A helicopter appears overhead, choppering out

toward the smoke, followed by another and then another. I suck in a breath and Adam and I look at each other before he turns and walks over to Rick, standing next to the ruined camper, a two-way radio to his ear. Most of the crew stops what they're doing and watches the helicopters circle the swamp.

Rick gets everyone's attention, holding up his radio. "Listen up! There is a wildfire in the swamp."

The chef peeks out from the dining tent, a serving spoon in his hand, moving to the shore of the lake in front of Rick where the rest of the crew has gathered.

"We are not in danger," Rick continues. "The park rangers are working with emergency crews to assess the situation and will communicate any updates to us. They've assured me that with the winds out of the south, it is unlikely we will require evacuation."

The crew goes back to their jobs, reluctantly, watching the smoke billowing on the other side of the water. I can't stand there any longer, the smoke swirling and changing, the helicopters not going away. So I help the chef with teatime snacks, help Laura feed Pudding a fish, and organize a few of the junk boxes in the prop tent. I think about Ronnie and

Theo, replaying the scene from the other day in my mind. Why did I have to lie to them like that? I basically ruined my chances of ever being their friend. I remember the look on Ronnie's face when she realized Survivor Guy was a fake. Total betrayal. And, to be honest, I know that feeling. I felt that way when I saw the set for the first time too.

It's midafternoon and work has slowed for just about everyone. Adam has his weather radio on, and a bunch of us are sitting at the edge of the lake watching the smoke, listening for updates. One thing we know for sure is the fire has not been contained. It's spreading.

I'm letting the makeup lady practice her smoky-eye technique on me when Claire calls, "George? Do you have Isabel?" Her head is poking out of the medical tent.

Dad straightens up from where he was helping chop up the tree in our camper. They're letting him use a little chainsaw, as long as Samuel stands right beside him. "No. I thought she was napping."

Claire shakes her head. "Her stuffed animals are gone. Have you seen her, Ali?"

I scan the set around me, and the makeup lady

pauses to look too. "Nope," I say. "She's not over here."

"Isabel!" Claire calls. We listen. "Isabel Grace, come out this minute!" We all stand in silence, listening hard for Isabel's voice.

"Come out for an ice cream, Isabel!" Dad says, but we hear nothing except helicopters and birds and bugs.

Rick lets out a whistle and the workers drop their chainsaws. "Break time! Let's everyone keep an eye out for Isabel."

Claire joins Dad at the demolished camper, and together they pull fallen walls aside, upending beds and hammocks, looking where a four-year-old might hide.

"Can she swim?" the makeup lady asks, closing her box of supplies.

"Could she have walked into the woods?" Bianca asks.

Claire is yelling Isabel's name louder now, and I hear something in her voice that makes my lunch form a lump in my belly. I look up and see the sky is darkening. A haze closing off the sunlight. Even though the air is hot and muggy, my skin is covered in goosebumps.

"Isabel!" I call, walking toward the dining tent and looking in. It's empty. I peer under the tables, whistling and clapping, because I know that works for dogs. I know nothing about kids. "It's me! Alison!"

I walk out the back and look inside the medical tent. Isabel's hammock is empty. Her animals, which are normally all lined up neatly on the floor, are gone. The lump rises to my throat. "Isabel?"

And then I remember Pudding, the only other four-year-old on the set. I run to the animal cages, calling Isabel's name, passing all the other crew members, who are now also searching for her. The animal area is deserted of humans, but the animals are all out of their houses, fully alert inside their enclosures, agitated. Lucy the alligator is pressed against the side of her pool and the snakes have slithered to the top of their terrariums. Pudding is crouched over something in the middle of her enclosure. She has it in her paws and as I step forward for a closer look, I scream for the animal trainer. "Laura! Laura!"

Pudding is startled and retreats to her little house,

taking whatever she has with her in her mouth. It's one of Isabel's animals. Her favorite one, the black kitten that has a pink collar just like Pudding. And there's more—Pudding kicks out a mangled stuffed penguin from her house before disappearing inside. I taste bile in my mouth. "Laura!"

Isabel knows Pudding is actually a man-eating carnivorous predator, right? Don't they teach that to kids? Hasn't her mother taught her that?

And then half the people on set are here, Dad holding Claire back from launching herself into the enclosure. Laura running up behind them with her animal catcher suit and net.

Claire is out of breath, sputtering next to me. "Is that Penguin?" She grabs my arm. "Do you think Isabel went in there?" And then she's shaking me. "Do you think she went into Pudding's cage?"

Dad hugs Claire while the rest of us watch Laura step into her chain-mail suit and pull it up over her giant marshmallow protective gear and silently enter Pudding's enclosure. I can't look. I turn away, nuzzling my face into the nearest body.

It's Adam. "No way she's in there. Laura keeps the keys to the cages on her belt. There's no way."

His voice rumbles through his chest. And it reminds me of when I used to hug Mom super close, snuggled on the couch, while she talked to Grandma on the phone, her words vibrating my face. All of a sudden I miss Mom so much it feels like choking. Does she wonder if I'm okay? Does she care that Dad's not coming back?

Laura has secured Pudding by clipping her leash to a chainlink wall of her enclosure and is rustling through the mountain lion's little house in the corner. She tosses out one, two, three stuffed animals until they're all piled up on the ground in front of us. Claire lets out a sob. But there are no signs of Isabel or her body parts, and I take a breath of relief, pushing Adam away.

"She's not here," Laura declares, releasing Pudding and letting herself back out the door of the cage.

Pudding looks at everyone gathered around, sniffs Kitten, then picks it up with her teeth and drags it into her house.

TWENTY-SIX

For a few seconds, everyone just stares at the rest of Isabel's animals, not moving. Doesn't she know we're looking for her? Can't she hear her mother's desperate calls?

The crowd starts to break up, continuing the search. I'm pushing through a clump of people to look in the trees behind the animal enclosures when everyone's walkie-talkies start chirping emergency-beacon-style at once. "BEEP! BEEP! . . . immediate emergency evacuation of Lake Drummond and surrounding areas . . . BEEP! BEEP! . . . this is a mandatory evacuation . . . tune to channel nine for further instructions . . ."

Everyone freezes and listens. Except for Adam. "I told you, Dad!" he shouts. "We should have left as soon as we saw that smoke!" He's angry, bright red in the face. "I told you!" Rick shushes him, but Adam doesn't calm down. "All of this, for what? A show about what it's like to sleep in million-dollar campers in a swamp?"

Rick fiddles with the walkie-talkie, searching for channel nine, and then a second later a voice comes through the radio, "Survivor Guy, proceed to coordinates N 36°35'41.9", W 76°26'19.5" for evacuation by helicopter at sixteen hundred hours . . . please copy."

Rick holds the walkie-talkie to his face. "This is Survivor Guy. Copy." And then he looks at the rest of us. "Okay, nobody go anywhere. Those are our coordinates. Sounds like they'll land a helicopter right here." He checks his watch. "Sixteen hundred hours is four o'clock. That's fifteen minutes from now."

Claire cries out.

"Number-one priority is to find Isabel," Rick adds, and everyone goes in different directions.

"We'll look around the lake again," Bianca says softly to Claire.

She nods and then sits on a boulder, shaking, her head in her hands.

"Hold this for a minute." Dad hands me his walkie-talkie and goes to her and I pretend it's my own mom sitting there getting comforted by my dad. And they're more than a united front. They're together and in love forever and ever.

"Camp Dig . . . move for evacuation . . . proceed to coordinates N 36°35'41.9", W 76°26'19.5" . . . copy . . ."

I snap to attention because I know Camp Dig. That's Ronnie and Theo's camp.

A minute passes and the call comes through again.

"Camp Dig . . . please respond . . . we are under mandatory evacuation . . ."

"Dad?" I yell, but they are back to searching with an even greater sense of urgency, poking the brush with walking sticks, Jake beside them now, yelling for Isabel. I can't even look at Claire, thrashing through the bushes, her arms bleeding from the branches.

". . . evac by helicopter at 1600 hours . . . proceed to coordinates N 36°35'41.9", W 76°26'19.5" . . . copy . . ."

I check my watch. Time is running out, and it's just too much to take. A fire, a lost kindergartner, and now an entire camp in danger.

". . . Camp Dig, do you copy? . . ."

Why aren't they answering? Maybe their walkie-talkies are off? What if they don't have walkie-talkies? What if they're out of batteries? Someone has to go get them. Someone has to make sure they're not left behind. I sprint over to Jake, who's helping Laura shuffle the animals into their cages, locking them inside. She's folding blankets for them and squeezing them through the crate doors and I feel like throwing up. Will they be evacuated too?

"Jake, I need your help. There's a camp and the park rangers can't get ahold of them and someone needs to warn them—"

Jake and the animal trainer look at each other and then at the animals. "I have to help Laura load the animals onto the golf carts. We don't have much time."

I stare as they pull three of the smaller cages onto

the back seat of a golf cart, strapping them down. The birds and mice and snakes, all chirping and squeaking and hissing.

"The fire road is still open," Laura says, out of breath. "I'm going to try to drive them out of here. It might take me awhile." She clears her throat, looking over my shoulder at the smoke moving around the lake now. "But I should be able to bring the pickup back for these bigger guys. It's parked at the boat launch."

"I'll wait for you," Jake says, patting Lucy the alligator's cage. "Hurry."

"Jake, what do we do?" I say as soon as she drives away. "There must be twelve kids at that camp. They don't know about the evacuation."

"Ali," Jake interrupts. "Help Dad and Claire find Isabel. The camp will be fine. They'll get out."

But I'm still holding Dad's walkie-talkie, and I can hear that Camp Dig is not responding. They don't even know they're in danger.

"Dad!" I run across the set to where he and Claire are talking to a circle of crew members. "Dad!"

When I get to him, he grabs my arms. "Ali. Listen

to me. I need you to stay here with Jake and wait to be evacuated." He pulls me in fast for a hug and squeezes the air out of me. Over his shoulder I see the smoke. It's grown. A wall spreading around the lake, and the helicopters are dumping something powdery on the trees.

"Dad," I say. "I'm scared."

Claire taps Dad on the shoulder and all at once he lets go and they start toward the woods.

"Where are you going? Wait!" I yell after him.

"The helicopter will be here any minute. I'll be right behind you as soon as we find Isabel." And then they're gone, leaving Rick, Bianca, and me to stare after them.

The attempts to contact Camp Dig continue to crackle over the radio. The helicopter will be here any second. "Where's Adam?"

Rick looks toward the lake. "Searching for Isabel."

". . . please respond . . . Camp Dig . . . mandatory evacuation . . . proceed to coordinates N 36°35'41.9", W 76°26'19.5" . . . do you copy? . . ."

We look at each other. "I know where they are," I say. "I can warn those campers."

"No." Rick shakes his head. "You heard what your dad said. You stay here."

"But you can come with me," I plead. "They're just past that tree I was supposed to climb." East of the tree. That's what Ronnie had said. "We'll be back in time for the helicopter."

"No," Rick says sternly. "The fire road isn't safe anymore and the bog is at least a half-mile hike from here. There's not enough time."

"Stay here, Ali," Bianca warns.

"Why doesn't anyone think this is important?" I yell, surprising both of them. "There are twelve kids at least in that camp." I flinch as another helicopter blares past us overhead, toward the fire.

Bianca puts a hand on my shoulder, her camera turned off for a change. "It's not that we don't care, Ali. But at this point, it's just too dangerous. You need to get yourself out."

"Fine," I say. "*Fine.*" I stomp off toward the lake, looking for Adam, but he's not there.

They must know, right? Ronnie and Theo would definitely be able to smell the smoke, and if they left camp looking for firewood again, they'd see the haze and clouds of ash in the distance, right?

But my mind keeps going back to the what-if. What if they don't know they're in danger? That could mean twelve or more families that never get their puzzle pieces back. And that's a chance I can't take.

I wait until nobody's looking and dash into the woods.

TWENTY-SEVEN

I reach the bog and branchless tree easily, but Rick was right, a half-mile hike in the swamp takes longer than I'd thought. Not to mention my legs are tired, my muscles burning from sloshing across the muddy ground. I hear a helicopter and it sounds like it's overhead, although I can't see much through the canopy of trees. A shrill repetition of emergency signals sounds from the walkie-talkie, making me jump. My watch says it's nearly four o'clock, and for a second I feel weak with panic. What if I can't find Camp Dig? What if the helicopter doesn't wait for me? Why didn't I look harder for Adam? Or at least tell Jake what I was doing? I consider going back, but it's too late now.

I can see Lake Drummond far off in the distance between the trees and I know I can't get lost as long as I have the lake in my sights. But their camp is inland, deeper in the forest, and I have to leave its safety.

I call everyone's names—Isabel, Ronnie, Theo—as I run and heave for air at the same time. For some reason, I feel lighter now. I can do this and I don't even care that my too-small shirt is halfway up my belly, or that I have a wedgie from my cargo shorts. Nobody's watching, so nobody cares.

I'm pretty sure I'm going the right way, but my memory from that day I visited their camp is foggy. Why didn't I pay better attention? I stop to catch my breath. Something feels wrong. There are no signs of life here, no voices, no overturned rocks or footprints. "Ronnie!" I yell, and my voice disappears into the swamp forest. The helicopters are getting closer now, drowning out my shouts. If I'm going to get to Camp Dig in time, I'll have to move faster.

It's dark even though it's late afternoon, with the smoke now blocking the sun. I look for a landmark, something familiar that will show me I'm headed in the right direction. But there's nothing. This swamp looks the same no matter which way I turn. "Theo!"

If I could find the right tree to climb, maybe I'd be able to get a better look, even see the archaeology camp from here. They can't be much farther. I've been walking for at least five minutes. I can't see the lake anymore. Only trees. And I can hear the bugs. Chirping. Flapping wings. I smell damp. Mildew. Soil.

When the first yellow fly bites me, I flick it off. But I'm deep in the trees now, I realize. Their territory. And they're ravenous. There's three on me and then five and then I lose count because my legs start running. Seven to ten miles per hour. Betsy Sue said you have to move seven to ten miles per hour to outrun the yellow flies. I should be moving inland more, in a straight line, but the brush is so dense, it's easier to follow the deer path in front of me. Just follow the path.

And this is why I'm not the hero. I'm the kid who goes along with everything. Who follows the path already cut, even if it's not the right way. But I don't want any more bites, because they hurt, and what do you expect from someone who hides Pop-Tarts under her mattress? I run with my eyes closed, because somehow that makes everything hurt less.

It's the only thing that feels right when so much is wrong: California. Isabel. Survivor Son. Dad's new life without me. I run with my eyes closed so I can't see the swarm of yellow flies. And it works, until I hit a tree with my outstretched hands, my walkie-talkie dumping into the puddle at my feet.

The swarm is still with me, and their bites hurt worse. I flap and spin and hop and cover my face. But the reality is still the same. I've just run myself straight into the swamp with no GPS or phone or thoughts of safety. During the peak hours of the yellow flies, without my bug helmet. And now everyone looking for Isabel will have to look for me, too.

My walkie-talkie bleeps from the puddle and I lunge for it. "This is Survivor Guy . . . Camp Dig has arrived for evacuation . . . all members accounted for . . ." It's Rick.

"Copy . . . we're on our way," someone says.

"Rick?" I say, pressing the button to talk, but there's suddenly no light anymore. I shake it and try again, but there's no saving it. Not even when I pound it on the tree. Not even when I pull the batteries out and dry them on my damp shirt, all the while batting bugs away. And it's just another thing to add to my list of failures.

I don't let myself cry until I see the helicopter beat past overhead, slow down in the distance, and start descending onto what must be the set. It seems miles away. Then I don't just cry. I sob. Loud and ugly.

Because reality hurts the worst of all.

I stand there. So still. A statue of a girl who can't do anything right. Betsy Sue also said that the yellow flies would stop biting after a few minutes if you stayed perfectly still. And they do. They stop swarming me and drift off, looking for their next victim. I don't feel their bites anymore. Just a dull, numb throb from my skin. And I remember Betsy Sue said something else. That if I moved, even an inch, the flies would find me all over again. So, I stay frozen. Except for my eyes. I keep them open and watch the helicopter disappear below the trees.

Nobody will find me here on my little deer path in the middle of the Great Dismal Swamp. I'll just disappear like Grandpa. I call for help one more time, but my voice is gnarled and raspy from my run through the woods. Still, if I call long enough and just stay in one place, someone will have to come for me. Right?

Grandpa's book said that staying put and waiting for rescue is the best chance for survival. So that's what I'm going to do. It's official, I'm going to stay here until someone finds me. And I like this decision, because it also means I won't get eaten alive by yellow flies. And hopefully Dad or Jake will remember to bring me my bug hat when they come to my rescue. And a granola bar or something.

My throat is burning from all my yelling. I'll add a whistle to my pocket survivor kit when I get home. I will also add bug spray. Because even though the yellow flies are gone, the gnats are not, and they crawl into my ears and across my neck and dangerously close to my nose holes. I sneeze, swallowing at least three of them. Protein. That's what Grandpa would say.

I hear a helicopter circling above me but when I look up, I can't see it. The smoke has settled into the trees. Acrid, poisonous smoke. It smells like a campfire, but I know it's dangerous. Deadly.

It takes me a moment to realize the gnats are gone

now too. It's like everything knows to get out of the forest but me. So, I change my mind. I can't sit here any longer. I can't wait to be rescued. I can't let the fire find me first.

I need to run. To save myself. That helicopter is not leaving without me. I'm not going to just disappear like Grandpa. I reach for the walkie-talkie, banging the water out of it against the tree, but it's still dead.

I'm lost. In a wildfire. With no communication.

Something I read over and over again in Grandpa's guidebook floats into my head. "You are never fully lost if you have a compass to follow."

My compass.

I reach in my pocket and pull it out, relieved that it's still dry, and flip the cover open. The *Survivor Guy* set is on the shore of the lake, so if I can find the lake, I'll make it back. I push on my forehead, thinking. If Camp Dig was east of the branchless tree . . . then the lake would be . . . "Come on, Ali," I say to myself, trying to picture a map in my mind. "Think. Think." The lake would be . . . west.

I find north with the compass to figure out which direction I need to go and then I start running. I squint through the smoke, following my compass, rolling my ankle once in a hole, tripping several times over roots and branches, and creaming my shin against a fallen tree. But the pain is nothing compared to my fear of being stranded. My fear of what happens if the wildfire catches up to me.

I splash into water, ankle deep, then knee-deep, and I don't know if I'm in the lake or just another bog, but then the brambles disappear and I'm walking on soft ground. Peat. I've made it to Lake Drummond. My rescue can't be too far away. I stay in the lake where I'm in the open, and even though it's hard to run in the water, the bottom of the lake is less rugged than the half water, half land of the swamp.

I can hear it. The helicopter is so close, but my vision is obscured by the smoke and I can't see it. My legs are like Jell-O, and I'm breathing so hard, I can feel the smoke in my throat. But I can't slow down. I push myself harder, trying to run toward the sound, but running is almost impossible knee-deep in the lake, smoke taking over my burning lungs. I cough and sputter.

I always pretended that if I were in this kind of situation, a survival do-or-die, I'd be the doer who gets crazy powers of strength. I'd be the kid who lifts the car off the toddler or the girl who leaps across the five-foot crevasse to reach safety. It's what I tell all my friends. But the truth is, my feet are soggy and heavy and I don't have any crazy powers of strength. In fact, I have barely any strength at all.

Then, by some miracle act of the universe, the dense woods on the edge of the lake thin into a clearing. The *Survivor Guy* camp. And then I run, splashing, flapping, yelling for the helicopter to wait for me. I fall, dunking myself, my eyes stinging from the swamp and smoke. But it's okay. Because when I finally crawl out of the water, lightheaded from the effort, the helicopter is still there, blades beating, up on the shore.

TWENTY-EIGHT

Someone materializes in the smoke in front of me and I'm running so fast that I can't stop before we collide. We land hard on the swampy ground.

"I found Isabel!" It's a voice I recognize.

"Adam?" I say. He's pushing me off of him and I'm trying to untangle myself, but then we hit heads and my forehead pounds.

He grabs me by my shoulders. "She's stuck, Ali. I can't get her out."

The helicopter is so close. No more than half a football field away. I can see it. The sound of the propellers is deafening. Can they see us? Adam pulls me toward the ruined camper, where Isabel is stuck halfway through one of the tiny vents on the collapsed roof. She's sobbing, calling for her mother. Adam and I each take an arm and pull until she screams in pain. It's like we're in a movie, because all of this can't be real. And the world is shifty and unbalanced with the smoke and the helicopter and rushing wind taking all of the sound from the swamp, leaving only the dangerous thumping of my heart.

"Ali, you have to go and tell them we're here!" Adam says into my ear. "Tell them we need help!" Isabel is screaming now. How can they not hear us?

I start toward the helicopter so fast I trip over my own feet. Then I'm up, galloping toward the blinking lights, leaving Adam and Isabel behind, hoping I can find them in the smoke again, pleading with the universe that we all get out of this safely. But then the wind changes, the smoke whirling and swirling around me. The red blinking lights are moving, lifting upward, and it hits me like a wall of flames. The helicopter is leaving.

"STOP!" The smoke catches me deep in the throat, smothering my words. "WAIT!"

But the lights are getting smaller now and I know

they can't hear me. My eardrums beat with the sound of the helicopter's propeller even after it has flown away, its departure sending debris across my back and into my eyes and mouth. *They'll come back*, I say to myself. *They'll be back for us.* But when the sound of the helicopter is gone, I can hear something else.

Flames. Popping. Hissing. Devastating.

I'm back on my feet, queasy, faint, and blind, my arms outstretched, looking for anything. Adam. Isabel. The wrecked camper. There's a red glow coming through the trees now. The wildfire is here and I'm running through the black smoke, trying not to breathe it in, heat wafting from the woods. Hot enough to scorch a pizza.

"I can't get her out!" It's Adam and his voice is so different—desperate, unsure, pleading.

I change direction, following the sound of it. "Where are you?" I call.

"Here!" he shouts, and he's right in front of me. Two more steps and I'm standing next to him. "Let me crawl in and push her from below," Adam says, giving me Isabel's little hand.

"I missed the helicopter, Adam," I say, squeezing until she squeezes back, a faint pulse. The failure of everything, getting lost in the woods—missing the helicopter—settles into my chest with the smoke.

Isabel coughs and I hug her, pushing her face into my shirt. She's not screaming anymore. "Isabel?" Why isn't she talking? "Isabel, are you hurt?"

She coughs a hacking, damaging cough. There's a roar from the trees behind the camper and I can see flames, feel the wind of the fire. I yank at Isabel. "Adam, push!"

I don't know if he hears me but suddenly Isabel and I are falling from the camper, in a clump, hitting the ground hard. She's crying and Adam reappears and we're scrambling away from the fire, both of us trying to hold Isabel and run at the same time. We fall again and I pull Isabel from his arms, yelling over the wind and fire for her to wrap herself around me so I can carry her.

A floating ember sparks by like a falling star in slow motion.

"We have to find somewhere safe," I say, but I don't even know what that means when you're in the Great Dismal Swamp with a fire burning fast and furious.

"Mama!" Isabel pushes me away, coughing and lunging out of my grip.

"Isabel, stop it!" Are her eyes not stinging from the smoke? Can she not feel the heat in her lungs yet? A spark lands on her pink sleeve and I swat at her, putting it out. She eyes the smoking pinprick in her shirt and howls, taking off toward where the dining tent should be.

"Mama!"

"She's not here, Isabel. Stop!" But she's fast for a four-year-old and we're basically running blind. "You're going to hurt yourself."

I look over my shoulder and see that the crackling and creaking and rumbling is upon us, flicking its fiery tail on the camper.

"You're going to get us killed!" I scream, and I can feel Adam by my side, both of us chasing a kid with a death wish in the middle of a wildfire. And even though part of me wants to freeze and cry for help until someone finds us, the other part of me wants to survive this thing.

Isabel stops. "You're not allowed to say"—she coughs again, rubbing her chest—"kill."

I try not to take deep breaths of the hot and burning air.

"I don't feel good," she adds.

A bolt of fear shoots through my body, because I know from my books that it's the smoke, not the flames, that kill so many people in fires. I pick her up, spinning around, looking for something, anything. Could there be masks in the hospital tent? A flaming leaf lands in front of us and I stamp it out, Isabel sobbing over my shoulder. "Mama."

"We need to get to the lake," I say to Adam.

He takes off the button-down he's wearing over a gray T-shirt and tells Isabel to cover her mouth and nose with it, and we start toward where I think Lake Drummond is, at first walking, burdened by Isabel's weight, but then as the fire gets louder, I jog and finally run. My mind drifts to Claire and Dad and what they're thinking right now. I stumble into Adam, running beside me, then regain my balance and force myself to think of only one thing.

Survival.

We can't be too far from the lake, and I wish on

all the stars in the universe that I'm headed the right way. *Please let it be close.* Isabel wipes her nose on my shirt and then all of a sudden we're falling again. Hard. Over something hollow.

"Canoe," she says, and lets go of me. I hear her clamber into it.

I try to picture where the canoe was before the fire. Jake had just taken it out. But did he return it to the storage area back by the dining tent? Had I stumbled that far? Or did he leave it on the bank of the lake, where he wasn't supposed to? Adam and I each grab a side and pull it across the earth as I grope for the water with my boot. *Please let the lake be here. Please.* "You still there, Isabel?" I ask, uneasy now that she's not in my arms.

"Yup."

"Get low and don't move. Everyone put your shirt over your face," I say. Adam is silent except for his loud breathing.

Through my shirt, the air smells like a burn pile of wood and leaves and grass, and there's an orange glow all around us, flickering like a Halloween strobe light.

"We have to hurry," Adam says.

There's a splash and I feel water on my shins. But there's no time to celebrate. "Are there oars in there, Isabel?"

I feel her body move to the front of the boat. "Nope."

Probably lying in the mud next to where we found the canoe. There's no time to run back. Soft flakes of ash start to fall around us like snow and I grab Isabel's hand and pull her out. "Hey!"

"Get wet, you guys!" I shout. But they don't move fast enough. "Come on! Before something lands on you."

We roll and splash ourselves in the water, soaking our clothes through. It feels good, cool on my hot skin, but doesn't help my lungs or my watering eyes. We help Isabel back into the canoe, and then we float away from the bank.

TWENTY-NINE

With the fire comes a windstorm, sending waves of blistering heat in our direction. I splash water on Isabel, tucked inside the canoe, and submerge myself in the lake. The water is covered in a layer of soot, splashing into my face, sticking to my skin. Ash lands hot onto my head, probably burning holes in my hair. That's not going to be a good look, if I survive this mess.

The lake bottom sucks my feet in with each step and I'm thankful I'm wearing hiking boots and they're tied tight. I worry there's quicksand, and then I worry about muskies and longnose gars and—

"My eyes hurt," Isabel says, sitting up, teetering the boat from side to side.

Adam helps her put his shirt over her whole face. "Here. Hold it there."

She flops back into the canoe and I dunk my head underwater to get my hair wet. When I come up, I get a glimpse of the shore. It's aflame. Fire is licking the water, crawling onto the set. I push harder against the lake bottom, taking us deeper.

The smoke is black. Dense. Everywhere. I gulp some water from the lake and immediately spit it out. Am I losing it? It's like my body is taking over for me, my lungs desperate for relief. Even this far out, flaming debris surrounds us like stars. I tell Isabel to jump in.

"You'll be safer in the water."

A leaf lands in the canoe, smoking. Isabel scrambles out of the boat and into my arms, grabbing me by the neck. She wraps her legs around my waist and even though the water feels warm now, we're shivering.

"Let's stop here," Adam says, after we've waded out a few more feet where the water is chest deep, just far enough that I don't feel like my eyebrows are going to singe off my face.

I hate how he's so quiet.

We catch our breath and stare toward the shore. The fire is devouring Dad's camper and everything inside of it. My clothes, my cell phone, Grandpa's book. And then it moves across the walking bridges like a living, breathing thing that doesn't like to get its feet wet. Isabel whimpers into my neck. "Where's my mama?"

"With my dad," I say. Hoping it's true. "Did they make the helicopter, Adam?"

Isabel reaches for Adam and he takes her onto his back. "Your mom is a medic, Isabel. She's going to be okay no matter where she is."

I dunk my head under again, the tears coming, and for some reason I can't let Isabel see. I need to be brave for her, even though I've never been the brave one before.

Underwater, I picture my own mom, at graduation, when I wouldn't let her hug me after I got my certificate. I brushed past her to where Harper was standing with her family. And when Harper's mom leaned in and said congratulations, I hugged her instead. My face burns with the memory. I blamed

Mom for everything for so long. She probably thinks I don't even love her anymore.

Something thuds against my leg and I'm jolted back to the present. "Did you feel that?" I say as I resurface, water in my eyes.

Adam shakes his head. "Lots of fish in the lake."

I shiver. Isabel repositions Adam's shirt over her face. I feel woozy in all the smoke, my legs tingling. My lungs burn and my eyes tear. A flaming pine needle lands in Adam's hair. I smack it hard, putting it out.

"Hey!" he says. "What was that for?"

I smile, because hair on fire or not, it felt pretty good to finally give Adam a smack.

"We should flip the canoe over," I say. "We can hide underneath." Like our own little shelter.

I tip the side of the boat with both hands, but it wobbles back upright. Adam is just standing there, staring at the fire. Silent. I snap a finger in front of his face. "A little help?"

But he's not paying attention. He's watching the set disappear in a frenzy of smoke and flame. We hear the sound of trees exploding with the heat, whole branches on fire, debris flying into the lake. It's so fast. I just can't believe it. What if we hadn't found Isabel right when we did? What if we had walked the wrong way in the blind smoke and ended up in the woods instead of the lake?

"Lucy," Isabel says. "Pudding. What about my animals?"

"Laura got them out," I say. "I think." Ugh. I meant to only say that in my head.

But what if she didn't get them all out? What if there wasn't enough time? It's almost too much for me to bear. I shudder, picturing us sharing a lake with Lucy, the half-ton alligator.

"Did Jake get out?" I ask. "Does anyone know?"

Adam shrugs. "I'm not sure. My dad did, though. First chance he got."

Isabel covers her mouth again with his shirt. "But Pudding will get hungry, and what if she doesn't know there's a fire?" she asks, muffled.

"I'm sure he didn't mean to leave you behind," I say to Adam. "If he knew you weren't there on the helicopter—"

"Let's just tip the boat, okay?" he interrupts. And

with one big push, the canoe is overturned, and the three of us duck underneath.

Isabel coughs and cries from getting water up her nose and in her eyes, but it's easier to breathe here, out of the heat from the wind, protected from the ash raining down on the lake, coating the water.

We are safe. For now.

THIRTY

We're quiet for a while. All three of us, Isabel draped over Adam, me holding on to one of the canoe seats to keep it steady over our heads. My arms are starting to feel numb. My brain is blipping from one paralyzing fear to the next. What if the helicopters never come back? What if Dad didn't make it out? What if he did, and left me here? What if I never get to tell Mom I love her again? What if I die here and I can't tell her how I got everything wrong? Because I know things now. Things I was too stupid to see before. And then everything combines into one giant ball of panic, settling into my stomach, hard as a rock.

"Want to play a game?" I blurt out.

Adam stares at me, shifting Isabel on his back. "No."

Isabel doesn't even answer.

I can't just stand here bobbing in the lake. The water is so dark. It's nearly up to my chest and I'm exhausted. "When do you think it's going to be safe to move closer to shore?"

Adam lifts an edge of the canoe and I see that even though the fire is moving fast, it's still hot and dangerous on land, the smoke deadly, the wind scorching.

"Okay," I say. "So, not anytime soon."

I try not to imagine what might be floating around me. Try not to imagine what a swamp muskie bite would feel like, or what I'd do if Pudding popped up under the boat with us. I mean, where would an animal go during a wildfire? Straight to the water, right?

"What kind of game?" Isabel asks, whisper-quiet in the dark of our canoe cave.

I'm looking at the water around me, wishing I had x-ray vision to see through the chocolate murk. Is that a ripple? Did something just brush up against my leg again?

"Uh, how about twenty-questions?" I bounce in place, making little waves in the water, lifting my feet from the soft lake bottom. I wonder if there are leeches in the swamp. Or eels?

"I've got a question, Isabel," Adam says, his voice strained. "Why didn't you come out when everyone was calling you? Did you think it would be funny?"

I don't like his tone. "Stop." I reach for Isabel, who takes my hand. I pull her onto my hip. "It's not her fault."

"We could have been on that helicopter."

"But we're not," I say, holding her tighter. "You could have left. You chose to stay."

Adam plunges into the lake, staying under for a long time, and I hope he doesn't grab my leg or something to scare me. Because I'll kick. Hard.

"I didn't mean to hide for so long," Isabel says, her lip quivering. "But everyone started sounding so mad, like I was in trouble, and then when I wanted to get out, I couldn't because my foot was stuck, and . . . I just want my mom and George Kensington."

I picture Dad and Claire running from the fire, looking for me. Looking for Isabel. Overwhelmed by the thought of losing us. A sob escapes my throat.

Adam resurfaces, wiping his face. He won't look at me, at Isabel crying loudly into my chest.

It feels like my throat is swelling shut from the hopelessness of everything and I breathe deep through my nose, coughing from the smoke.

"Sorry, Isabel," Adam finally says, patting her on the back. "It's not your fault. It's not. I just . . . wish we were out of this place."

I look out from beneath the canoe and I see that the fire has blazed through the clearing, past the little canal with the walking bridges that divided the *Survivor Guy* camp in two, and is inching onward. I wonder how long we'll have to wait for rescue.

The set is a blackened pile of smoking debris. "I think we can move closer to the shore now," I say.

Adam turns around and stares through the gap at the destruction. There's no way anything could have survived the fire. I search the singed set for the animal cages, but I can't make them out.

I help Isabel move to my back and it takes Adam and me working together to flip the boat back over. Nobody talks. Isabel doesn't ask for her mother anymore. She doesn't protest when I put her in the canoe and we start walking through the water to shore.

"Everything's gone," she finally says.

The smell of burning overpowers us as we get closer. Adam secures the canoe into the muck near the shore and we climb in, the higher ground too hot, parts of it still smoldering. I lift a floppy Isabel into my lap. She's soaked and shivering, even though the air feels like a hundred degrees. I feel for the bandage on my head, relieved it's still there even after being in the lake.

It's the perfect time to say everything's going to be okay. That rescue will be here soon. That we'll get reunited with Dad, and Claire, and drink milk-shakes and eat french fries as we drive away from the swamp.

But I'm not lying anymore. Hiding the truth doesn't help anyone.

So I pull her closer and push away the matted hair from her eyes.

"Want to know why it's so great you get to skip kindergarten?" I say.

She stirs but keeps her face hidden in my arms, sniffling and hiccupping.

"Finger painting," I say, getting a look from Adam. "Because there's always that kid in your class who eats it or smears it on your favorite light-up shoes or gets it in your hair. And then before you know it everyone loses their finger-painting privileges. It's not fair."

I don't have the heart to tell Isabel that kindergarten was all parachute games and reading chairs and new friends. And when I got off the bus at the end of the day, Mom and Dad would both be there, because *Survivor Guy* was still new and exciting and had barely any viewers. That's when Mom still thought Dad was funny. We all did.

Isabel looks up at me, her eyes swollen. I put the shirt back over her mouth. The air is still sharp with smoke.

"And if your mom gives you your favorite kind of cookie in your lunch box, like with extra chocolate chips or something, the teachers make you finish all of your vegetables first. Even if it's your birthday."

Isabel cries into my armpit. "I love extra chocolate chips."

The swamp is gray and still, the wind gone with the fire. It's dark even though it's barely past six o'clock and the sun won't set for another couple hours. Adam and I exchange a glance when we hear a rumble of thunder in the distance.

"You're lucky, Isabel," I say. "I bet your tutor will

let you have all the finger paints and cookies you want." But really, I'd do anything to go back to when life was all about Play-Doh and coloring and getting grossed out when your parents held hands. When, if you made your best friend mad, you gave her your favorite sticker and went right back to being best friends forever. I never knew how good I had it.

A flash of lightning puts all three of us on high alert and I think of the storm from last night. Wild. Violent. Is that how everything is in this swamp?

"Just a summer storm," Adam reassures Isabel. "That's all."

The rain starts slowly and at first we ignore it, Adam and I singing songs to Isabel to distract her, and it's working, especially when we do "Wheels on the Bus," the Dismal Swamp edition. Adam is so good with her, making her laugh, getting her to sing with us. I wish that his dad had waited for him on the helicopter. Stopped it from leaving until we were safe aboard. I wish that his dad hadn't left him four years ago.

We're in the middle of "the alligators in the swamp go CHOMP CHOMP CHOMP" when we realize this storm isn't just passing over. Thunder echoes, shaking the earth, the sky pulsing with lightning. And with each flash we get a better glimpse of the devastation, and it's like we're on some other planet where the ground is dust and the trees are skinny scorched toothpicks.

Adam stops singing. "We can't stay here." He stands up, looking at the sky, even though it's impossible to know the difference between a storm cloud and a smoke cloud.

"Where do we go?" I say, because he's right. We're basically sitting in a giant pool. One lightning strike and we could all be electrocuted.

THIRTY-ONE

We step delicately onto the shore, pulling the canoe behind us up onto the bank, our clothes dripping. "Ow!" Isabel yells when I lift her out of the boat and put her on the ground. She drops Adam's shirt. I grab it. The ground is still smoldering in places, even with the rain coming down, and I step carefully around the hot spots. The wind sends sparks into the sky. "My foot hurts. Owwww."

"Where?" Adam asks over the noise of the storm. "Can you walk?" He tries to inspect her foot.

"Ow! Don't touch it!"

She must have injured herself when she was stuck in the camper.

There's a crack of lightning so close I feel the tingle of electricity in my body.

Adam scoops Isabel up. "Hang tight. We need to find shelter now," he says, cradling her like a baby.

I step over a downed tree, scared I'll see a scorched animal. Or worse. We stand together for a minute, looking, thinking. The rain picks up fast and hard.

"No," Adam says, seeing me eyeing the camper debris. "Too much metal. Probably still hot from the fire too."

There's nothing left of the dining tent or the circle of crew trailers or the prop tent. The cottage is gutted, the roof caved in, and the screened-in porch is gone. The entire set is deserted. Annihilated. I notice that, oddly, some of the trees look barely touched, except for missing leaves and blackened bark, almost like the fire moved too fast to eat them whole. When I look up, I see that some of the tallest trees even still have their green canopies.

"I might know of a shelter," I say. "I mean, if it's still there and . . . if I can find it." I feel around in my pocket and pull out my compass, shaking the water off it, rubbing it with my hand. For a second I don't think it will work, and I'm surprised that there's no water inside of it. But the needle holds steady, pointing north.

Adam shifts Isabel higher on his chest. "Know how to use it?"

I'm not sure of anything except that Camp Dig is east of the branchless tree, which may not even be there anymore. And even if it is, without all the brush and leafy branches all around, what if I don't recognize it? We won't have any of the normal landmarks or a golf cart to get us halfway there. And maybe the woods aren't even safe yet. What if the fire starts up again with all this wind? But the sky is ominous, black and dangerous. I know one thing for sure, we're not safe out here in the open, right next to a giant lake, in a massive electrical storm.

The rain drums against my body, the wind giving me chills.

"Let's go," I say, and this time I'm not going to play it safe, because what do we have to lose?

With no other real choices, we step into the smoking woods.

Soot. Ash. Blackened trees. The once lush green and brown landscape is gray. Colorless. Lifeless.

"Do you know what you're doing?" Adam says when I hold the compass out. Isabel is quiet.

"Stop asking me that," I snap, taking the lead. "Just follow me."

Most of the underbrush is gone. Skeletons of ash collapse as we walk through. The trees that are still standing are marked with burns, and smoke has settled between them like fog.

"Watch for signs the fire's gone underground to the peat of the swamp," Adam says. "It'll look like a lot of smoke and crawling flames. Very dangerous."

We walk, Adam moving Isabel to his back, his arms probably numb from carrying her. We try to ignore the desolate forest. We try to ignore the rain pelting us in the face and the wind blowing soot into our eyes. At least there are no yellow flies to worry about anymore. In fact, not counting a burned snake we tripped over when we first started out, there are no animals at all. It's like we're the only living things in the entire Great Dismal Swamp.

The storm whips through without mercy. We're

deafened by the rain and the wind and the thunder. I think I hear a helicopter, but then I look up and only see the cloudy black skies. There won't be a helicopter until the storm passes.

I walk fast, retracing my steps as best I can to where my branchless tree should stand. When we come to what looks like an area that used to be a clearing, I pause. Could this have been the place? My stomach twists. The trees are now nothing more than steaming stumps. What if we get to Camp Dig and find our shelter had the same fate?

A crack of lightning makes Isabel scream, the wind swirling ash into our faces.

"Ali," Adam says.

"Okay. Let's keep going." I trust my gut and follow the compass east. I ignore Adam's nervous chatter about peat fires and broken bones and dangerous rescue missions. I ignore the swamp water squishing in my shoes and between my toes.

"Over there!" I call.

Camp Dig is far off to the left, not exactly on our path, but with the forest so gutted, what's left of it is easily spotted. The thunderstorm is nearly on top of us now, the trees swaying, creaking. The rain is torrential. We run, splashing through swamp puddles, tripping over blackened roots.

The camp looks as ravaged as our set. Some of their metal tools survived the wildfire, scattered across the ground. The lines protecting their precious dig are dust. Tents have been consumed. I pick up a small shovel and it's still warm.

"Wow," Adam says. The bones of a sun shelter remain, the plastic parts melted and disfigured. A pot sits on a stump, ready to make the next meal, like nothing happened. Isabel looks up, but the rain is coming down too hard and she curls into Adam's back. I wish she wasn't so quiet and I wonder if we should have been more careful getting her unstuck from the camper.

"This way," I shout.

We stumble to the big tree that Ronnie showed me. The one with the giant roots sticking out of the ground, hoisting it up to make the perfect shelter for someone who needs it. I'm relieved it's still here. Blackened and leafless, but still standing. I pull on one of the woody roots. It's solid. And I know a tree that's probably a hundred years old like this one has survived a storm or two before. Maybe even a few forest fires.

"You want to seek shelter in a tree during a lightning storm?" Adam says, stepping back, wiping rain from his eyes.

"I'm cold!" Isabel hugs him tighter.

I look up. It may be the thickest one around, but it's definitely not the tallest. There's a cluster of trees towering over it. "Safer than a lake or an open field."

I pull Isabel off Adam's back and we crawl under together.

"Ow!" She pauses over her foot, sucking in a breath.

"Go slow," I tell her. "Be careful."

"It's dark, Ali!" she says, reaching for me, trying to get out.

"I'm right here." But the darkness makes me catch my breath too. My little glow-in-the-dark watch says it's not even seven, but the clouds of smoke have blotted any signs of daylight out of the forest. I grope the ground with my free hand. It's smooth and dry. But what if we aren't the only ones to seek shelter in the tree? Just a few hours ago the swamp was crawling with all sorts of creatures—alligators, snakes, spiders. Where have they all gone? I picture the ghosts of the people who used this shelter in the past sitting beside us in the dark, and I have to pinch myself back to reality.

Isabel is holding my body so tightly I'm practically choking. I manage to get us squeezed into a comfortable spot, away from the driving rain, and I pull her into my lap, stroking her hair like my mom did when I had to get stitches in fifth grade. We used to snuggle all the time when we were watching movies, sharing a blanket and a bowl of popcorn—no butter, of course. But not since she told me Dad was moving out. After that, I wouldn't let her touch me, not even to braid my hair for the sixth grade sing-along. And I didn't care when she looked hurt. Because I thought she deserved it.

"Hold on a sec, guys," Adam says, climbing in next to us. I shift over to make room, but even when I'm squashed into the side of the tree, I can still feel Adam's legs on me, and my nose gets hit with something.

"Ow!"

"Sorry, sorry . . . okay, there." He's sitting finally, probably with his legs crossed, because his knees are touching my arm. I pull away, wrapping it around Isabel.

A moment later a light flicks on and at first I think it's lightning. But he's balancing a flashlight upright, digging it into the dirt in front of us, illuminating our little shelter. I feel Isabel relax.

"Did you just find that?" I ask. My back is getting wet from the rain sprinkling in through the roots. I'm realizing the earth isn't completely dry in here either, and my butt is getting soggier.

"Must be from the camp." Adam scoots closer to me and Isabel. "Let's take a look at that foot."

"No!" Isabel shrieks. "Don't touch it!"

Adam looks at me and I shrug. "Maybe it's safer to keep it in her boot?"

We angle the light to take a closer look, and we see it at the same time. The red creeping up her little pink sock. Blood.

"Hey," Adam says to Isabel, untying her shoe, which is ripped and shredded at the top. "Did I ever tell you the story about when my dad and I found a secret—"

"—hot tub in the woods?" Isabel finishes.

"Yes, the hot spring, and we were walking and walking trying to find this waterfall—"

"—but you never found the waterfall," she says.

"We had this map," Adam says to me, loosening the laces super slow and careful. "It was some kind of Boy Scouts thing, and we were supposed to hike to the waterfall, but we got lost." He picks at a knot. "And we were about to turn around when we stepped into this clearing, and right there was this hot spring. Totally natural. Totally in the middle of the wilderness."

Isabel yelps as Adam tries to pull off her boot and I hug her tighter.

"And then what happened, Isabel?" Adam asks.

"You went in the water in your underpants!" she says, but not in her normal pink-frosted-doughnut-with-sprinkles kind of way. Thunder vibrates the ground.

"We sat in there for an hour. We even missed the shuttle back home and had to call Mom to come get us."

"Your real dad or your stepdad?" I ask.

He stops tugging for a moment. "My stepdad. I don't have many good stories with my real dad."

"I don't have a real dad," Isabel says, and for a moment I'm sputtering in a tidal wave of shame at all the times I'd been so mean to her.

"Real dads aren't always the best kind of dad," Adam tells her, and with a final gentle pull, he gets her boot off.

"Ow ow ow ow ow ow . . ." Isabel reaches for her foot. I hold her hand and Adam takes off her wet sock.

It's a bad cut and I cover Isabel's eyes. "You are so brave, Isabel," Adam says. "I don't think it's broken, and it's not really bleeding anymore. Do you still have my shirt? Can I use it to wrap up your foot?"

She stiffens.

"Hey, have I ever told you the story about when I went to New York City with my dad when I was eight?" I ask, trying to quiet her cries, rubbing her arms against the wind that whips into our shelter.

Adam takes the shirt from Isabel and, with his teeth, starts ripping it into strips.

"We took a train there and I got to wear a fancy

dress, like one of those kinds made out of sequins, you know? It was blue green like the ocean, and he put it in a box and stuffed it under my pillow. He likes to do that, put things under my pillow for me to find."

"One time George Kensington put a glittery rock under my pillow and it was probably a diamond," Isabel says, watching Adam wrap her foot in what's left of his plaid button-down. "And then what happened?"

"And then when we got off the train, there was a limousine, a big extendo one, and Jake was so mad that he couldn't go. But it was just me and my dad that night. It was for an awards show and I was Dad's date." I think for a minute and wonder if that was the last time Dad took me on one of his Daddy-daughter dates. When I was little, we used to do that kind of stuff all the time.

"Wow," Isabel says. "It's like you were famous."

It was probably the only time I was in the newspaper with my dad without a Pop-Tart hanging out of my mouth or something.

"I still have that dress," I tell her. "It's a little big, but I'll give it to you if you want."

Isabel sits up so fast, Adam almost drops her foot. "Really? And do you have high heels? Because I'm really good at walking in high heels."

I laugh. "Maybe we'll have to go shopping for those."

"Yes!" She does a little shimmy.

And for a second it's like we forget we're huddled under a tree in the middle of the swamp, muddy, wet, and injured.

"There," Adam says. "Done." He double knots the shoelace he tied around his shirt-bandage. "Feel better?"

Isabel nods her head. The storm is finally passing. I can't feel the rain against my back anymore, and the thunder is fading to a distant rumble.

The ground beneath the tree is cleaned from the work of the archaeology camp, a few little holes scattered around with red flags indicating important finds. Isabel finds a pail of brushes and picks and shovels by one of the tree roots. She jangles the tools inside the pail, the sudden clatter in the silence of the forest surprising us. Because besides the drip-drops of rain, it's like a ghost town out there.

Adam reaches for a flag. "What are these for?"

"Don't touch that!" I say. "It's a marker for really important stuff."

Isabel digs a little hole and inspects it with a magnifying glass.

"From people who lived here a long time ago." I take it from his hand and put it back where it belongs. "Like maybe hundreds and hundreds of years old."

He looks around our little hideout. "How do you know?"

"Ronnie and Theo told me. They gave me a tour of their camp." Regret warms my face. I wonder if I'll ever hear from them again. "They were looking for evidence that people used to hide in the Great Dismal Swamp. Like, people who escaped slavery." And then I whisper, "And I heard from a little old lady that there might be some ghosts too."

"What did you say?" Isabel asks, straightening up, still holding the magnifying glass to her eye.

"Creepy," Adam says.

"What's creepy?" Isabel nuzzles close to me. "Do we have to sleep here?"

"Don't worry, Isabel. Adam's just being a baby."

But my skin is all goose-pimpled. It's one thing to be in the middle of a place like this with a chef and a stunt lady and a million-dollar camper. But to be out here alone in the wild with whatever else—living or not living—calls this place home is a different thing. A different thing entirely.

"I'm hungry," Isabel says, dropping her pail, the contents scattering on the ground.

I dig into my pocket for something—anything—to distract her from her stomach grumbles, but all I find is an old, swampy peppermint candy. I hold it up, frowning.

"I love those!" she says, clapping her hands.

We watch her rip it open and pop it into her mouth and then listen to her lip-smacking noises, ignoring our own stomach growls. According to the chef's menu, dinner tonight was supposed to be spaghetti and meatballs and extra-buttery garlic bread. My mouth waters.

But then a howling sound breaks the quiet of our shelter. Loud and long—and close.

"Pudding?" Isabel says, lunging for my lap.

Adam and I are on full alert. "Mountain lions don't howl, do they?" I ask.

He's quiet, still listening. We hear the howl again. Closer?

"Wolf," Adam says.

And then, right at that moment, the flashlight batteries run out. We plummet back into the darkness.

THIRTY-TWO

Isabel is practically hyperventilating. Her candy drops onto my leg, sticky.

"Isabel," Adam says, "Isabel, it's going to be okay. It's only dark."

But Isabel is not okay, wailing, screaming. I've never been in such complete darkness before either. And maybe it's her screams that make the wolf go away, because there are no more howls, the forest back to silence except for us.

"We're safe in here, Isabel. Safe." Adam is trying to get the flashlight back on. I can hear him smacking and shaking it.

"I guess it's bedtime," I tell Isabel. "Do you normally sleep with a night-light?" I pretend it's just another day camping in the wild, time to hit the hay after our bellies are full of s'mores and our minds full of campfire stories.

Not ghosts. Deadly wildfires. Man-eating predators. I want to throw up.

"Aren't you tired?" I ask, as Isabel finally quiets. I want to tell her that when we wake up, we'll go home in a helicopter. That her mama will be waiting for her. But I can't promise any of that. So I say, "We've had a really full day. We should sleep."

"I'm thirsty," she says, hiccupping and digging herself into my lap again. Adam sits facing me, both of us cross-legged, our knees touching. "Can I have some water?"

"Soon." I feel the dryness in my own throat, raw and tight from coughing so much. "Close your eyes. Get some rest."

I recite what I can remember of *Where the Wild Things Are*, stopping and repeating the part where Max tames all the wild things on the island. It's the part that Dad always liked the best too. He'd read it over and over to me and Jake, sitting together on the couch, Mom upstairs laying out our pajamas and putting toothpaste on our brushes. A working, functioning family.

Isabel is quiet at the end of the story. Something touches my hand and I jump.

"Just me, sorry," Adam says shyly.

But he doesn't pull his hand away. He squeezes mine and then we sit in the dark like that for what feels like eternity, the silence pounding in my ears. I try not to think about how this is the first time I've ever held a boy's hand.

There's no amount of sleep in my body. Not even after all the running and bobbing in the water and hiking through ravaged woods. Not even when I've had nothing to eat or drink for hours and hours. How can someone sleep when you don't know if your brother and father are safe? If you have no idea if you'll be lucky enough to be rescued? If maybe you're being hunted by a wolf or a mountain lion dark as midnight wearing a pink collar?

"Adam?" I whisper.

Isabel is out—her breathing raspy and loud—and I wish I were her, sleeping through this horror story.

"Adam, are you awake? Adam?"

"Yeah."

"Can you sleep?"

"Nah."

My head is aching under my bandage. Maybe from lack of water or from all the smoke I inhaled, or maybe because I've been listening so hard for whatever danger might be lurking outside of our shelter. Adam lets go of my hand and slides beside me. Isabel stretches, and Adam pulls her legs into his lap and I cradle her head. Our own little family.

"Do you think they'll wait for us?" I say. "The helicopters? It will take us awhile to get back to the set."

"Of course."

"I mean, our dads must be so worried."

He snorts. "Nah."

"What do you mean, 'nah'? Of course they're worried."

"My dad doesn't care. I'm only here because the court said he has to spend time with me. Part of the deal when my parents got divorced."

My stomach tightens. "Dads always want to spend time with their kids. It's part of nature," I say quickly.

I don't want to talk about this anymore. "You think there will be another storm?"

Adam rubs his arms. The temperature is dropping in our little tree shelter, and we're still damp from the rain.

"Not nature for some people, actually. This is the first time I've seen my dad in four years. He's always on a shoot or traveling. You know the deal."

"Nope, not really," I say. "Don't know that deal at all."

"My mom finally got fed up and took him to court again. The judge said he had to take me this summer."

I picture Mom and Dad in the Jeep in our driveway, arguing, and how Mom told Dad he never spent any time with me. But, four years? I don't know what to say, so we just sit with this bubble of silence between us.

"I'm starving," I finally blurt out of nowhere, startling Adam. "Where's the chef when we need him, right?" I force myself to laugh, but it hurts my body, and I end up coughing. Isabel stirs, then goes back to sleep.

"Jake said your parents are divorced, too."

"Separated," I correct, thankful for the darkness all of a sudden.

I feel him move a little, his legs shuffling on the dirt floor as he tries to get comfortable.

"Separated? Or divorced?" Adam says. "Because there's a big difference."

He doesn't have to tell me that. Separated means there's a bitty light of hope left that they'll stay together. "Doesn't matter anyway, since he's moving across the country."

"You didn't know that was happening?"

I shake my head, even though I know he can't see.

"Jake said he tried telling you a thousand times. That you never wanted to hear it."

"No, he didn't."

Adam sighs. "I know how you feel. It's like if someone doesn't say it out loud then it's not really going to happen."

I'm holding my breath, trying not to cry.

"Or pretending something isn't true that's really actually true," Adam goes on. "That's not exactly lying, you know."

Now he's just being nice to me, and I wonder, when did that happen? "Of course it's lying."

It's what I'm so good at. What makes me just like my dad. I lie to my friends at school about being the next Survivor Girl, and to my dad about archery awards that don't exist, and to my own best friend about my parents. It's like I don't even know how to tell the truth sometimes.

"Actually, they've been divorced for three months," I say, not even whispering it, declaring it loud and clear to whatever man-eating predators are out there. Because maybe I don't want to follow in my father's footsteps. Maybe I'm done with all the lying. "And also, I suck at archery."

Adam laughs, and then I'm laughing too. And maybe it's just the fact that I haven't eaten for twelve hours, but I've never felt lighter in my life.

"Do you ever feel like you might have everything wrong?" I say. "Like how it is with your dad. Like maybe your dad's not completely the bad guy all the way?"

I hear him sigh. "I don't know. Pretty sure when you leave your own family, that makes you the bad guy." He shifts, our shoulders now pressed together. "And then out of nowhere after four years he wants to pretend he's my dad again." He snorts.

"Like, *wabam!* he's back?" I say, and Adam snickers.

"Yeah, like, *wabam!* And, the problem is, my stepdad is awesome. Really, really awesome. So what if I'd rather spend the summer with him, you know?"

I move Isabel, her head lolling onto my shoulder. She's warm and I hold her closer, rocking her back and forth.

"Don't worry," he adds. "Your dad's not all bad. Maybe at being a Survivor Guy, but—"

I punch him in his shoulder. But after a few seconds, I say, "He's not the Survivor Guy I thought he was. I always thought everything was my mom's fault. I thought she was causing all the problems and my dad was working so hard."

I wait for Adam to say something mean about him again, but he's quiet.

"I actually thought he was changing the world. Teaching people how to survive in the wild. Saving lives. Like my grandpa did."

"Well, maybe he did teach you something," Adam

says. "We survived a swamp fire on our own, didn't we?"

I think about this, wondering who gave me my survival instincts. Because, actually, it was my mom who gave me all those books. Took me to used and rare bookstores all the time to find cool survivalist books you can't buy in regular stores anymore.

"*Wabam*," I say.

"*Wabam*," Adam says back.

We pass the rest of the night telling truths about ourselves—how Adam secretly respects my dad, how he doesn't know if he'll ever be able to forgive Rick, how he's afraid of snakes, and that his middle name is Rooney, not Jonathan. I tell him that I always thought *I'd* go into the family business, not Jake, how I'm not the greatest best friend in the world to Harper, and that it was me, not Michael, who flushed the sock down the toilet in school causing the Great Toilet Flood in third grade.

Eventually I think we drift off, Isabel, Adam, and me all clustered together under our tree, Adam and me leaning our heads against each other. The swamp and the fire are still there when I close my eyes, and I can't tell if I'm awake or dreaming. Sometimes I think I hear a helicopter, or the howl of a wolf, or even my mom's soft whisper. It's hard to sleep because my throat burns from the smoke and the thirst. And just as the sky is starting to lighten up and I'm finally falling off into real sleep, a sound pierces through the forest. It's not a howl or a snarl, or even a helicopter.

It's a whistle.

THIRTY-THREE

"*They came back* for us!" I'm up so fast, I toss Isabel onto the dirt floor.

"Ow!"

Adam is halfway out of the tree already. "They're looking for us."

"Mama?" Isabel crawls out and tries to stand up, a layer of soot on her face from yesterday's ordeal, but Adam hoists her onto his back before she can put weight on her foot.

I scramble out after them, and then we're running away from our shelter and into the Dismal Swamp, back toward the set, leaping over fallen trees and dodging debris. The whistle comes every few seconds and Adam tries to respond by whistling through his fingers, but it's not loud enough.

"We're here! Wait for us!" I call, but my voice cracks, hoarse from the smoke. I try again and again. We will not be left behind this time.

Adam stops. "It's not coming from the set."

We listen.

"We're going the wrong way," he says.

"No." I shake my head. "The helicopters can't land anywhere else."

"It's coming from over there." Isabel points into the distance. But it sounds like it's coming from everywhere, bouncing off the leafless trees.

"Maybe we're not the only ones who didn't get out," Adam says.

We walk, carefully now, all of us listening, afraid our crunching through the scorched woods will drown out the sounds of whoever's out here with us.

"We're walking deeper into the swamp, away from where the helicopters will be," I say nervously. "That whistle could have come from anywhere. We'll never make it back in time. They won't know we're here."

Adam stops. "Should we just go to the set? Hope whoever is whistling will make it there too?"

We hear the whistle again, and it's closer. We're heading in the right direction. Adam takes off toward the sound, Isabel getting bounced and jiggled all over the place. I jog after them, kicking up soot and cinders.

The whistle is louder now, more insistent. Isabel yells, "Zip-a-dee-doo-dah!"

We hear a faint "zip-a-dee-ay" back, and I can't believe it, my body nearly giving out, my knees tingling, and I can't run fast enough. Adam and Isabel disappear through a cluster of trees. I sprint, tripping over a log but managing to stay upright. When I catch up to them, Adam is standing over the gully where I hit my head. Where we taped a scene of *Survivor Guy* like it was no big deal just a few days ago. Claire is hurtling herself out of the ravine. She runs straight for Isabel, sobbing and panting, her clothes muddy and soaked. "Isabel," she chokes, pulling her from Adam's back into a trembling embrace, Isabel wrapping herself around her mother, calling, "Mama, mama, mama . . ." over and over, like she can't even believe it's her.

"Where's my dad?" I look around, panicked.

"You're hurt?" Claire says to Isabel, checking her

all over, pausing at the blood-soaked wrapping on her foot.

"He's over here!" Adam shouts, pointing into the gully.

I run to the ravine, dropping to my butt to slide down the side. Adam is already in there, next to Dad, who's propped against the muddy wall of the ditch, unmoving. "Dad? Are you okay? Dad?"

"Do not move him!" Claire yells, following us into the gully with Isabel on her hip. "It's his leg. Don't touch."

His leg is in a splint made out of sticks and ripped-up pieces of netting from my bug helmet. He's pale. Breathing too fast. And sitting in a shallow pool of water that's collected at the bottom of the ditch.

"George Kensington?" Isabel says shakily.

He opens an eye. "My girls."

"They're okay, George," Claire cries, her face mud- and tear-streaked. "They're okay."

"How did you—" I can't find the right words, looking all around, taking in the scorched forest. "But, the fire—"

Claire pats me on the back. "When it caught up to us, we had nowhere to go. We just started running. We didn't even see the gully until George fell in." She fidgets with the bandage on his leg. "Obviously we didn't avoid injury completely, but the fire passed over us."

Dad's trying to get up, to hoist himself off the ground.

"Stop! Wait, George." Claire hands Isabel to me. "Adam, help me get him upright. We need to get him out of this gully and back to the set before the helicopter comes."

They try to lift him up, but Dad is silent, limp, foggy. How are they going to get him out of here?

Isabel pulls on my shirt and points off to the horizon, and then I hear the sound of a helicopter approaching. Our rescue. And we're still in the middle of the swamp where they'll never find us.

"Helicopter! Helicopter!" Isabel shouts.

Claire and Adam look at each other, still holding on to my dad, but barely able to move him. The wall of the gully is too steep. He moans.

"Claire," I say. "How bad is it?"

She looks at me, helping Adam sit my dad down again, propped up against the side. "You really want to know?"

I exchange glances with Adam. "Yes." I need to know the truth. No matter how bad.

"His leg is broken in several places and he's going into shock." She wipes her nose. "He has a rapid pulse, and it's weakening. We need to get him out of here."

Everyone watches as our helicopter, our rescue, flies over the lake and lands, disappearing into the woods.

"Mama! It's going to leave without us! Mama!" Isabel is hysterical, and I can barely hold on to her flailing body.

Claire takes her, shushing her, holding her tight.

"You guys go to the helicopter. I'll stay here with Dad," I say.

Adam crosses his arms. "Yeah right, like we're leaving you here alone."

Claire paces the gully, her boots splashing through the water. "We need to stay together." She stands firm in front of me.

"If we stay here together, they'll never find us." I look at my dad. "If you don't go now, none of us will be rescued."

"Mama, it's going to leave us!" Isabel cries again,

struggling out of Claire's arms and landing hard on her injured foot. And we can see that it hurts, but she doesn't even stop, clawing her way out of the ravine. "Please, Mama!"

"I'll go. Adam, you stay here," Claire says, scrambling up after her.

"No," I say. "The set is pretty far away. What if you get lost? Nothing looks the same since the fire."

"Alison—"

"Number-one survival rule is to use the buddy system. I stay with Dad, you guys go together." I hand Adam my compass. "Take this with you."

They're all staring at me, and then looking at Dad.

"If there's anyone with the skills for sitting and waiting and doing nothing, it's me," I say. "No stunt double required." I try to laugh, but nothing comes out.

Adam studies me seriously for a second.

"Let her do it," he says.

Claire sighs, looking at me for a long time, her face creased with worry. But then she nods. "Someone will be back for you in twenty minutes, tops. Keep your dad still."

Adam and I climb out of the ravine together.

Claire kisses my forehead. "I'm proud of you, Alison." Isabel gives me a hug from her mom's arms, and then they're gone. I watch them until they disappear into the torched swamp. Adam turns to wave goodbye one more time, holding up the compass. "*Wabam!*"

"*Wabam*," I say quietly. Then I slide back down into the gully and sit with my dad, putting his head in my lap, trying not to look at his battered leg.

For a moment he opens his eyes, and then, just before he drifts off again, he mumbles, "My Survivor Girl."

THIRTY-FOUR

I'm sitting and waiting and doing nothing, just like I said I would, relieved that Dad doesn't seem to be in too much pain, relieved that I can see his stomach moving up and down with each breath. He's breathing so fast. But at least he's breathing.

With each crackle of leaves or branches moving in the wind, I wait for an animal to appear above us. We're so deep in the gully I can't see anything from here. Nothing except for the blue sky and some green treetops that were high enough to escape the fire, as if nothing happened to this Dismal Swamp. As if everything is as it should be.

It's been so long, I'm sure Adam and Isabel and

Claire have reached the helicopter by now. I strain to hear the beating of its propellers, but it's too far. I hear nothing. And I feel like we're the only two people on this whole entire earth. My heart pounds with the emptiness.

Dad stirs, wincing, his eyes watering.

"Don't move, Dad. You'll hurt yourself worse."

He stops, but his body is tense.

"Does it hurt really bad?" I ask.

He moves his head up and down, slowly.

"They'll come for us soon. Don't worry."

"I put everyone in danger, Ali," he says, opening his eyes. "We had nothing for fire protection."

"How could you have known?" I say. "You can't predict a forest fire."

"It's June, Ali." He tries to sit up, but I stop him. "All it takes is one lightning strike. That's it."

"It's not your fault, Dad."

"I have thirty people working on set. They trusted me," he whispers, each word a great effort. He shakes his head, and are those tears in his eyes? Or maybe it's just from the pain?

"Dad . . ."

"Reckless."

"People love you though, Dad. They love the show. That's what matters. That's what you've said all along." Now's not the time to talk about this. As angry as I am about what this show has done to our family, about the lies and the separation, he's still my dad.

He groans, reaching for his leg. "If they love me for being someone I'm not, do they really love me at all?"

His words hit me in the gut.

"I don't want to be remembered as a fraud."

Clouds are moving in and clumping together, and a streak of fear runs up my spine because it almost looks like smoke. The sun is gone.

Dad is drowsy again, dozing off, and I lift his head from my lap and gently slide out from under it. I kick a boot into the soft earth, pushing myself halfway up the gully wall to peek at the swamp around us. I strain to listen and hear a faint beating sound in the distance. Is that the helicopter? Does that mean the others have been rescued? And we'll be next? I look back at Dad, sleeping now, pale and sweating.

I climb up the muddy wall and an unnatural heat settles over me. When I look out, there *is* smoke in the distance, inching toward us. I don't see flames, but there's a creeping red glow, close to the ground, moving like lava.

Peat fire.

Just like Adam said. The fire has gone underground. And we're directly in its path. A tree falls in the distance and I watch in horror as it catches fire after hitting the ground.

"Dad!" I dive back into the ditch, half sliding, half tumbling. I shake him and he barely stirs, flapping his eyes open for only a second before drifting off again. "Dad! The fire's back!"

I'm spinning around, looking for anything that can save us. How long do I have? Where can we go? How far to the lake? I grab Dad by the arms, pulling them over his head, trying to move his dead weight. He jerks awake, the movement agony to him. "Dad! You have to help me! The fire!"

I get close to his face. "You're Survivor Guy, Dad. You can get us out of here. What do we do?"

He's quiet.

"What would your writers say to do?" I'm yelling at him, shaking his shoulders. "What would Grandpa do?"

There's a loud THWAMP! and the ground vibrates. Another tree fall. The peat fire must be eating the roots of the trees.

I grab Dad under his arms. "We have to get out of here. Help me!"

But I can't even budge him from his spot in the mud. And I know I'm running out of time, my face burning not just from panic but from the heat of the fire. I try gripping his hands, pulling his arms over his head again. We move an inch. I pull again and Dad shrieks with pain, but we move another inch. I pull faster and harder, ignoring his screams. Can someone die from the pain of a broken leg?

The gully is filling with smoke. I cover my mouth with my shirt, but I need both hands to pull, so I let it fall from my face and try to take shallow breaths. The smoke envelops me, and I feel claustrophobic. I can barely keep my eyes open, the smoke stinging and burning. I pull Dad toward the puddle in the middle of the gully that I hope will turn into a creek and lead us to the lake.

The splint Claire made for his leg starts to unravel. I stop to tie the netting tighter, reposition the sticks so they'll stay. We need to move faster. "Dad, can you use your good leg to lift your body off the ground when I pull? Ready?"

He's quiet, not really talking, but the next time I slide him toward the watery ground, he bends his good leg and helps push. We move almost a foot, my eyes tearing from the smoke. I can't believe this is happening.

The earth is getting muddier, slippery, and it's harder to find footing and pull Dad through the muck. And the gully is too narrow to risk staying put, too close to the fire that has reignited around us, no longer creeping, but leaping into flames. I tug at him again and again and again, blocking his yelps from my eardrums, hoping Claire can fix him up, knowing the fire will mean certain death.

The muck becomes a puddle. I drag him through it, in the direction I think the lake should be. And the puddle turns into a bog. The bog a stream. Chocolate water, our savior.

When the water is up to my waist, I try to float Dad next to me, but he's kicking his good leg, dragging his bad leg on the floor of the creek, and can't relax and lie back. I heave his weight onto my shoulder and I count each step, telling myself I can take one more, my muscles threatening to collapse. The water is deeper, almost to my chest. Our gully is now a narrow interior ditch. We must be getting closer to the lake, and yet the fire seems to have grown; the heat feels unbearable on my face. I worry that as the wind picks up, the flames will be able to reach us. So I keep us moving.

"Dad?" He's not answering.

It's hard to keep him above the water. He's slipping from my shoulder and I'm not strong enough to hoist him onto my back.

"Dad, on the count of three hold your breath," I plead. He doesn't respond. "One!... Two!... Three!" I dunk us under the water and maneuver him onto my back, pulling his arms over my shoulders as we come back up, sputtering, spitting. I stagger. He is so heavy, his whole weight on my back. I take slow steps, wondering how the rescuers will find us now that we've moved. Wondering if I will have to sleep another night in this Dismal Swamp. How will I ever get us through this?

The flames are smaller now, burning out around us, the fire moving on. But the smoke is thick and choking.

And then suddenly, the water becomes too deep to keep my footing, the muck beneath me falling away. I lurch forward, the weight of my dad pushing me under. I can't find the bottom of the ditch again. It's like a giant hole has opened up underneath us and I'm kicking at nothingness, holding my breath, my lungs burning for air. I try to roll Dad off my back, but what if I lose him in the chocolate darkness? I pinch him hard in the side. Kicking. Flailing.

I pinch him again, and I feel the weight on my back lighten, just enough to get myself oriented, put a foot on the soft swamp floor and stand upright. But Dad is thrashing, his body still submerged, unable to stand on his damaged leg. I grab him, hoist him up, and reach for a thick root sticking out of the side of the ravine. He's coughing. We're both coughing. Gagging on the smoke-filled air.

"Leave me here," he whispers.

"Never."

And then he drifts into unconsciousness again, his eyes closing. And I'm Survivor Girl. One girl, no camera, miles and miles of unforgiving wilderness.

I just wonder how this episode will end.

THIRTY-FIVE

I move more carefully now, slower, spooked from our near drowning and dizzy with thirst and fear. Dad is so still, I can finally float him on his back. I hear a splash in the water up ahead. My knees weaken and I bring him closer to me like he can offer some kind of protection.

"Isabel?" he says, eyes still closed.

"Ali. It's me, Ali."

There's another splash, and I picture a thousand-pound alligator swimming toward us. And I have nowhere to go, the banks of the ditch still glowing with fire, Dad in no condition to help.

The smoke is thick and has settled on the water, making it impossible to see more than a foot in front of me. But I hear the splashes getting closer. Rhythmic. It's a good swimmer, whatever it is. I take steps backward, pulling Dad with me. But, really, what's that going to do? Delay the inevitable by a second?

I scream. It's loud and shocking in the quiet of the forest. Dad flails in alarm. "Ali?"

"Hello?" someone calls from the smoke. "Is someone there?"

"Me! Me! I'm here!" It's a human. An actual human voice and not a man-eating alligator. "Help!"

The tip of a rowboat appears in front of us. "We're right here!"

"Are you with *Survivor Guy*? Are you injured?"

I see a face now, wearing a white mask.

"My dad," I say, keeping him afloat with one arm, latching myself onto the boat with the other so it can't go anywhere. "My dad has a broken leg. He needs to get out of here."

"We've been looking for you." The man opens up a bag and pulls out two more masks. "Put these on."

I take one and slide the other over Dad's head. His eyes are still closed; he probably doesn't even know we're getting rescued. We get him in the boat first, the man hauling him up by his arms and me cradling his legs. I get pulled in behind him. The man lays Dad out on the floor of the boat as best he can and covers him with a foil blanket. I sit on the other plank seat with a foil blanket of my own, shaking even though I feel warm. The man hands me a granola bar and a jug of water, but it's like I forget what I'm supposed to do with them.

"Is everyone safe?" I ask. "The little girl and her mom? Adam? Jake?"

He pats his walkie-talkie. "Heard they landed a few minutes ago. Had trouble getting them out with the fire restarted."

"What about everyone else on the helicopter yesterday?"

"Fine, other than supremely worried about the rest of y'all."

Relief. I move my mask to take a drink of water, feeling the coolness all the way to my stomach. "Can you tell them my dad needs an ambulance?"

He nods. "Already taken care of." He whips out the walkie-talkie and says, "Heading back with two survivors." I cough, my eyes watering. Survivors.

"I'm Robbie-Jay, by the way," he says, turning the boat around and paddling us through the smoke.

"Glad I found you guys. The fire's gone out of control. In the peat now."

I straighten. "Robbie-Jay?" I open up my foil blanket, showing him my shirt. "Like this Robbie-Jay?"

He slaps his knee. "Well, I'll be darned. Mama said that was y'all lost in the swamp. She knew it. Said you had no preparations for this wild place."

"But—she gave me your bug helmet, and said you had it on your last day," I tell him. "I thought you were dead."

Robbie-Jay laughs. "Yessir. Wore it on my last day. My last day as assistant to the assistant park ranger, that is."

"You weren't attacked by a bear?"

"Nope."

"But—"

"Saw a bear once or twice, though." Robbie-Jay paddles us out toward Lake Drummond, where the smoke is less dense. "These parts are chock-full of animals. Nothing like the Great Dismal Swamp." He clears his throat, his eyes gliding over the destruction. "Nothing like it."

I watch the swamp pass as we move along the water, out of the interior ditch and across the lake.

So much devastation. Just a few days ago, this place was a jungle of green and yellow. The lake alive with fish, the air buzzing with black and yellow flies. And now, everything is so quiet. The trees are mostly black picks sticking up from the soot-covered ground, a few of the biggest and tallest ones still sprouting green leaves at the top, a reminder of what it was like before.

"Did you know these waters are healin' waters?" Robbie-Jay says, lifting a paddle, the water running off it. "Olden days, folks used to come fill jugs of it to cure their ailments. Thought it cured everything. Great-Grandpappy cured his foot fungus with one soak here in the lake."

I grimace.

"With time, these waters'll do their job, you just wait. Heal this place good as new." He sniffs. "Good as new."

But what if there's so much damage, not even time can heal it? I think with an ache in my chest. Then what?

I nibble on my granola bar, watch Dad to make sure he's breathing, and sip the water. Much of the swamp is hidden by smoke, but as we round out of the lake and into the small canal that leads back to the boat launch, I think I see something. The smoke is thinner here, the brush still intact in some places. I look into the woods again, searching, and there she is. A black mountain lion standing on the bank of the lake, partially hidden by the trees, her pink sparkle collar unmistakable.

I open my mouth to say something to Robbie-Jay, but she's off with a flick of her tail, pouncing back into the swamp.

Her swamp. Her freedom.

THIRTY-SIX

"You've got some buddies back at the launch," Robbie-Jay says as we finish the long paddle up the canal, the end of our ordeal in sight.

I touch Dad's head. "We're almost there." I can see the boat launch where we first entered the swamp. It seems so long ago.

"Got treated on site for smoke inhalation because they all refused to go without you to the hospital." Robbie-Jay smiles. "And a few others who were rescued last night. Argued they had to be here in person to see you two come out safe."

We paddle into the boat launch area, where the trees are full of leaves and wildflowers are popping up through green grass, untouched by the fire a few miles away in the swamp.

We come to a stop with a thump against one of the dock bumpers. Jake is there, hand outstretched to pull me out of the canoe. And I'm so surprised and relieved and happy to see him that I nearly burst into tears. Behind him, Claire waits on the grass next to Rick and Adam, Isabel in her arms. There are at least three fire trucks, four ambulances, and just as many police cars in the small parking lot. My foil blanket drops into the water and someone fishes it out for me and someone else hands me a new one, and part of me thinks I'm still in the swamp during the fire and I'm dreaming. Have I been eaten by an alligator? Is this the afterlife?

Jake hugs me tight. "Glad you're a better Survivor Girl than a soccer player."

"Archery."

"I know, I know," he says, squeezing me tighter.

"Do you think Mom knows what happened?" I push away from him, my eyes stinging with all that I have to say to her.

A rescue team shoves through us to get to Dad

before he can answer me. They're moving so fast and I wish I could ask them if he's going to be okay, but my mind is buzzing and numb, and my hands are shaking, spilling my water bottle.

They put Dad on a stretcher and his eyes flutter open for a minute. Just enough for him to smile at me. Jake runs with the rescue team to the ambulance. And then an EMT takes my elbow and we follow behind them and I sit in my own ambulance—in the open-doored back of it, not on a stretcher—and they replace my little white mask with a heavy plastic one that sounds like breathing and spits out a fog that tastes sticky-sweet. I close my eyes for a second and when I look up again, Adam is there, pulling my blanket tighter, sitting next to me. And the memory of the last time I sat on the back of an ambulance washes over me: Harper's seventh birthday party at the fire station.

I jump when the ambulance next to me turns on its siren. It drives away and my heart beats double time because I know it's Dad in there. Adam squeezes my shoulders and I wipe my eyes.

And then Claire is kicking Adam out and sitting next to me, hugging me so hard my mask gets knocked off. "I'm so proud of you, Ali. You put your own life in danger to save your dad. To save Isabel. Thank you. Thank you," she repeats again and again, until the medic in her takes over and she checks my eyes and listens to my heart and holds my wrist while she whisper-counts to herself. She peels off the old bandage on my head and swaps it out with a clean one.

"Your dad's going to be okay," she says when she's done. "They're taking him to the local hospital and most likely they'll medevac him to a bigger one. He'll need surgery on his leg. We already know that."

I spot Adam back by the canal, next to Rick, and are they standing closer together than normal? Is Adam laughing?

"Isabel?" I ask, my voice muffled behind the oxygen mask.

"She might need a few stitches on her ankle," she says. "The EMTs checked her out and gave her crutches until we get to the hospital. She's never been happier."

"And the animals?"

Her smile drops. "Saved all but one." She looks at the ground, wiping her forehead. "They had to leave Pudding behind."

Adam is walking back up to us, orange juice and a white paper bag in his hand.

"I think she'll be okay," I say.

Isabel hops across the grass on her crutches and Adam stops in front of her, reaching inside his bag and pulling out a giant chocolate chip cookie. Isabel squeals and hobbles off with it.

"There's this little old lady with pastries over there," Adam says, squeezing in on my other side. "I've already had like three cinnamon rolls." He hands me the juice and opens up the bag, revealing giant pastries.

I take it from him, reading the stamp on the front. SWEET TREAT BAKE SHOP, NOT EVERYTHING'S DISMAL IN THE GREAT DISMAL SWAMP. "Look!" I point from my muddied and bedraggled shirt to the bag. "That's the lady that gave me this shirt! Betsy Sue! Robbie-Jay's mom!"

"Where'd you meet her?" Adam asks, taking a bite of doughnut.

I sip my juice and put my mask back on. "It's a long story."

We watch Isabel as she hops off a rock one-legged on her crutches, holding her cookie.

"She said you told her the Wild Things story until she fell asleep." Claire takes a chocolate éclair from the bag. "That's her favorite book."

"Mine too," I say. "When I was her age."

"Well," Claire says, "I just hope you and Adam know that what you did last night—and Ali, what you did today—was just amazing."

Isabel bounces over. "Can I have another cookie, please please please? Look, I'm an eagle!"

She flaps her crutches like a massive bird, balancing on one foot and nearly taking out an EMT who gets too close. "I don't think that's how you use crutches," I say.

"You've had enough cookies, little one," Claire adds.

Isabel grabs my hand. "Do you want to come live with us in our new house?"

I look at Claire. "New house?"

"Being on the *Survivor Guy* crew was a great

experience, but"—she pulls her daughter into her lap, her crutches falling to the ground—"I've got more important things to think about. Like kindergarten." She kisses her on the cheek.

Isabel makes a gross-out face and immediately wipes it off. "I'm not a baby, Mom, I'm like five years old."

"You're four."

"I'm almost five."

"I haven't told your dad yet," Claire continues, "but I think it's time to settle in. Get a regular kind of nursing job. This medic will only be available for shoots during school holidays and summer vacation."

I smile. "Maybe we can have a sleepover later this summer, Isabel."

She grabs my face, her hands sticky with cookie. "But in a bed," she says seriously. "Not in a tree."

Adam and I laugh. "Deal."

The sun and sugar are starting to wake me out of my brain fog.

And soon I'm not even shaking anymore and I take off my blanket, but the medics dabbing ointment on the many scratches on my arms and face insist they're taking me to the local hospital to be checked out, just to be safe.

"Come on," Claire says. "We're all going." She hops down to find Isabel.

Before I get up to climb inside the ambulance, Adam bonks me with his shoulder. "You're the real deal, Ali."

I smile, starting to feel like myself again. And I'm pretty sure I have cinnamon roll on my face, and probably even on my nose, if we're being realistic.

Adam hands me a napkin. "Don't you ever forget it."

THIRTY-SEVEN

When we get to the hospital, we wait in the hallway to be seen by the doctor and rechecked for smoke inhalation, and for Isabel to maybe get stitches. I'm on a chair next to Isabel's gurney, where she sits quietly now, and Claire and Adam wait in their own chairs beside us. The quiet makes me worry about Dad, and just as it starts to feel like too much, there's a ruckus outside the ER entrance. A car squealing into the parking area, stopping right up front and nearly taking out one of the benches along the sidewalk. Claire stands up for a better look, but I don't have to because I'd know that car from anywhere.

"Be right back," I say, and before the EMT or

Claire or anyone else can stop me, I'm off my chair and running across the waiting room.

The doors open and Mom steps through in her high heels and conference suit and I almost knock her over with my hug. A hug to make up for lost time. A hug to make up for not paying attention. For avoiding the truth. When I finally pull away enough to look up at her, she has tears in her eyes.

"I came as fast as I could," she says. "I couldn't get a flight, Ali. I slept in the airport, waiting. I just—"

"It's okay, Mom," I say. "I did it. It's okay. I survived."

"And your father?" She looks around the waiting room.

"They're flying him to a bigger hospital for surgery."

I hug Mom closer, and I can't hold back anymore, hot tears spilling down my face. "I love you. And I missed you so much. And maybe you were right and I wasn't ready for all of this."

She smiles and shakes her head. "I've been talking to Jake. He said you were incredible. That you saved Dad's life. Imagine if you hadn't been there."

I take a shaky breath, still not letting her go. "Do you still love him, Mom? Even if you're divorced?"

"Always, Ali." She rubs my back. "Always."

Outside, the sun is getting lower, and an ambulance races off to another emergency. I know everything's going to feel different now. And that maybe we won't be like that family on TV making Friday-night homemade pizza dinners and eating our slices picnic-style in front of a movie. But maybe now that I've lived through two forest fires and a deadly storm, having two parents who don't live in the same house but probably still love me just as much doesn't seem like the crisis it did a few days ago.

We find out from the receptionist that Dad's been transported to a hospital close to home in northern Virginia. Claire and Isabel are going to drive to a hotel near the hospital so they can see him in the morning after his surgery. Mom waits with me as a doctor checks my throat and lungs and oxygen levels. And then we wait for Jake to come back from the cafeteria, where he went with Rick to get Adam something to eat. At last, Jake, Mom, and I leave the hospital and climb into our own car.

Adam waves to me from across the parking lot

where he stands with Rick. He has something in his hand. I run to him, not sure if I should give him a hug or just say goodbye. But when I get there, he says, "Don't forget this," and hands me back my compass. "Still works. It's like indestructible."

"Thanks," I say. And I hug him. I don't even mean to; it just happens. But he hugs me back.

"See you again sometime?" he asks. Rick joins us and puts an arm over Adam's shoulder, kissing him on the head.

"Definitely." I walk backwards toward Mom and Jake. "And just you wait—I'm going to have muscles bigger than yours!"

"Is that a threat?" he calls, rolling up his sleeves and showing me his biceps. "*Wabam!*"

"It's a promise!"

Jake grabs me by the elbow, pulling me across the pavement as he waves to Adam. "Come on, lovebird."

"What?" I'm offended. Highly offended. "I'm not in love with Adam!"

"Sure, Ali." He opens the back door for me and I climb inside.

The sun is behind the trees now, and I slump against the window. Mom drives us away from the hospital and the Great Dismal Swamp, Jake talking about bear claws and fishing rods and falling trees. And I'm happy not to talk at all, letting my eyes close, holding tight to my compass, dreaming of soft beds and best friends.

THIRTY-EIGHT

The next morning I'm up early, banging on Harper's door. Her mom answers, and I push past her and run up to her room, flinging myself onto the Harper-size lump in her bed. She opens up one eye and then bounces awake. At first, it's like we were never in a fight— we're hugging and she's asking if I'm okay and how I got back and telling me how she was hearing about us on the news. But then she remembers. I can see it on her face and in the way she pulls her blankets up tight to her neck.

I take a deep breath. "My parents are divorced, Harper, and I wasn't even admitting it to myself and that's why I never told you." I have to take another deep breath from the words coming out so fast. "And my dad is actually just an actor on a show that's supposed to be reality but it's not." She blinks at me from her blankets. "And I told everyone at the *Survivor Guy* set that I'm awesome at archery."

Harper crawls out of her covers and sits next to me on the edge of the bed. "I knew all that pretty much." She stretches. "Except for the telling everyone you're awesome at archery part, which is pretty hilarious."

"He has a chef on set," I say. "An actual chef that makes homemade pop tarts, and we slept in these millionaire campers. It was really crazy."

"I saw you on the news. Your picture. When you were missing."

"Oh, God, what picture did they use?"

"Don't worry about it." Harper laughs. "I tried to make my mom drive us to the swamp, but she said no."

I look down, feeling light with relief. There's a puzzle dumped out across her floor. "You're going to lose some of those pieces."

"I hate puzzles," she says.

"Well, you like the idea of puzzles. You always start them, but never finish."

I can't help myself. I lean over and inspect a piece, looking for its spot in the half-put-together picture of a sunflower field.

"That's a pretty big bandage on your head," says Harper. "Were you really in a forest fire? Where did you sleep?"

I find one of the end pieces of the puzzle and snap it into place. "Yeah. Under a tree."

She looks at me, wide-eyed. Even after all the truth I just told her about my lying, she doesn't doubt me. And that's why Harper is such a good friend.

"I don't even know how to describe it." I think of Adam and Isabel and my dad, and I know that even if I don't see them every day, there's a special thing that we'll always share. Something that even my best, closest friend will never understand. It almost makes me feel a kind of lonely I've never felt before. But then Harper sits on the floor with me and helps me finish the puzzle. Even though she hates puzzles. It's missing three pieces in the end.

"Doesn't always have to be perfect," she says. "See? You don't need all the pieces to see the picture."

And maybe best friends don't have to understand all the pieces of you. "Do you want to go to the hospital with me to see Dad?"

Harper slides into her ducky slippers with the annoying squeakers. "Pancakes first, with celebration chocolate chips and whipped cream."

"Hold the whipped cream," I say, standing up. "I'm trying to grow some muscles."

Harper snorts and I punch her in the shoulder.

Later, when Mom, Jake, Harper, and I get to the hospital, Dad is sitting up in bed, his leg in a cast and elevated by a big pillow. He's watching *Me in the Wild* on TV. Jake jumps away from the television like he's been shocked. "How can you watch this guy? He's terrible!"

I lean in and give Dad a kiss and he hugs my neck, not letting go for a long time. "Couldn't be more proud of you, Ali-Gator. You saved me back there. And Isabel. And Adam too."

"I'm so glad you're okay, Dad."

"You're so much like your grandpa," he tells me.

I straighten, pulling out of his hug. "I lost the

book. His guidebook." It's part of the swamp now. Soot. Ash.

"You don't need that anymore." Dad smiles. "Plus, you still have his compass, right?"

"Wait, you mean—" I feel around in my pocket and pull out the compass. "This was his?"

He takes it, flipping it over in his hand. "Each of these little scratches has a big story behind it." He pops open the cover. "When I was a kid, he always had this with him. Every time we went fishing. Every time we took a hike or went on an adventure." He hands it back to me. "I found it in some of his things a while back and I thought you should have it."

I snuggle in next to him on his bed and we watch as the guy on TV breaks open a hazelnut with his bare hands and downs the meat inside. "Survival," he says, breathless, "is keeping your nutrient levels up."

I shake my head. "Do you think this guy has a prop tent too?"

"I heard he films half of his shows in a secret Hollywood studio," Dad says, laughing and then wincing from the pain.

I wonder about Ronnie and Theo, and picture

them back with their own families, telling them all about how Survivor Guy and his daughter are just big frauds. I know they're right, but part of me still wishes I could talk to them one more time. Apologize.

Harper knocks over a pile of boxes of chocolate, and one of them bursts open, sending smooth brown squares across the floor. "Sorry!"

We rush over to help her clean up, Jake mourning each lost piece.

"I bet this was a caramel one, my favorite," I say, tossing it toward the trash can, and it bounces off the wall and rolls back to my feet. Harper shoots and makes it. "Showoff," I say.

When I turn around, Mom and Dad are whisper-talking, and I feel the bubble in my stomach like always. The maybe-bubble. Like maybe this is when they'll fall back in love with each other. Maybe this will be the time they decide to stay married.

But then Mom stands up. "I'm going to get us some coffee from the cafeteria. Anyone want anything?"

We shake our heads. My maybe-bubble pops, and it hurts my entire insides for a second.

Jake and Harper open another box of candy, trying to identify all the chocolates inside.

"Hey! I found another caramel. Want it?" Jake calls to me.

"No thanks." I sit in a chair next to Dad, gagging a little when I look at his leg and the pins and bandages and gauze.

The guy on TV is weaving a blanket out of leaves now. Leaves and ivy branches. I picture his own producer handing him already-sewn-together leaves off camera, a crew of ten people standing behind him.

"What's going to happen to *Survivor Guy*?" I ask.

Dad clears his throat and takes a sip of water. "Don't know yet. But there's going to be big changes. We'll have to delay California a bit while we figure things out."

He's still going. I take a deep breath, the smell of hospital cleaner and chocolate and cold oatmeal from Dad's breakfast tray filling my lungs. But at least he's not going right away.

"Part of the deal is you're going to spend summers with Jake and me," Dad says. "We'll be home for holidays and you can visit us anytime, and in the summer, you don't even have to come on set if you don't want. I can delay tapings or take breaks if you'd rather that."

"And Jake will officially move out of our house?" I ask, my stomach dropping.

"I know you'll miss him." Dad pats my leg. "But this is a big step in the right direction for Jake. He needs to start thinking about his future. He's an adult now."

Jake pops three candies into his mouth, licking melted chocolate off his fingers and rubbing his hands clean on his shorts.

Dad laughs. "Okay, *technically* he's an adult."

There's a commotion in the hall, a pounding, flip-flopping sound, and I know it's Isabel. And then she's crashing into the room with a dozen or more balloons, all of them getting stuck in the door frame. I leap off my chair to help her, and when she sees me she lets go of the balloons and runs in for a hug, sending them all floating out into the hallway.

"I got 'em!" Harper says, and there's a frenzy of activity as everyone helps collect the runaway balloons.

"I got new underpants for kindergarten!" Isabel

tells me, completely oblivious of the commotion she's caused.

I give her a squeeze. "I missed you already, Isabel."

And then she springs onto Dad's hospital bed, captivated by the *Me in the Wild* guy chasing a giant turkey through a field on TV.

When Mom comes back, she has a full tray of coffees and hot chocolates. I see her hesitate when she spots Claire and Isabel, but half a second later, she's back to smiling and probably nobody even noticed except for me.

And maybe Jake, who stands by my side.

"You must be the famous Isabel," Mom says to Isabel, shaking her hand.

"I'm five." Isabel holds up her hand. "And I have new underpants."

"She's four," Claire corrects from where she sits by the windows.

Mom grins. "Well, but it looks to me like you're almost five. At least."

Isabel nods vigorously.

"Mom, she can have my hot chocolate," I offer.

"Oh! I knew we'd have more visitors this morning, so I got extra."

She hands them out and then we all sit around Dad: Claire and Isabel, me and Harper, Jake and Mom, sipping our warm drinks in the cool hospital. Mom and Claire talk about the terrible coffee, Jake and Dad roll their eyes at Wild Guy's attempt to start a fire, and Harper puts an arm over my shoulder, showing me her hot chocolate mustache. "Think I'll get a date to the middle school dance?" she says, fluttering her eyes.

"Who wants to see my new underpants?" Isabel asks, standing up.

Jake tickle-tackles her off the bed before she can flash us or fall over onto Dad's leg.

"Inappropriate, Isabel," Claire scolds, trying to be serious, but she looks at Dad and they can't help but laugh.

And when I look at Mom, I see that she's laughing too.

Isabel's balloons are scattered around the ceiling and I think about how, even though my parents aren't together anymore and Jake is moving across the country, somehow it feels like my family is bigger than before. It's far from perfect. And there are definitely some pieces missing in our puzzle. But maybe it's like Harper says. You can still see the big picture through all the missing parts.

"Fine!" Isabel flings her arms out in surrender, knocking over Jake's hot chocolate.

And then everyone is up, Harper and Jake nearly hitting heads to stop the spill from spreading, Claire reaching over and plucking Isabel from the scene, and Mom whisking her own coffee out of the way.

Maybe it's weird, but I'm kind of liking how all the pieces are coming together. The maybe-bubble in my stomach starts to feel more like a hope-bubble. Because through swamp fire and lightning strikes, and even across thousands of miles of country, this family just might survive.

McKenzie Co. Public Library
112 2nd Ave. NE
Watford City, ND 58854
701-444-3785
librarian@co.mckenzie.nd.us